MR. WAHLQUIST
IN YELLOWSTONE

MR. WAHLQUIST
IN YELLOWSTONE

DOUGLAS H. THAYER

PEREGRINE SMITH BOOKS

SALT LAKE CITY

First edition

93 92 91 90 89   5 4 3 2 1

This is a Peregrine Smith Book, published
by Gibbs Smith, Publisher, P. O. Box 667,
Layton, UT 84041

Manufactured in the United States of
America

Design by J. Scott Knudsen

Cover illustration by Royden Card

**Library of Congress Cataloging-in-
Publication Data**
Thayer, Douglas H., 1929-
   Mr. Wahlquist in Yellowstone / Douglas
Thayer.
        p.   cm.
   ISBN 0-87905-339-9
   I. Title.
PS3570.H346M7   1989
813'.54—dc20   89-4023
                                    CIP

The paper used in this publication meets
the minimum requirements of American
National Standard for Information
Sciences—Permanence of paper for Printed
Library Materials, ANSI Z39.48–1984 ∞

For My Father

TABLE OF CONTENTS

Acknowledgments

"The Rooster" originally appeared in *The Colorado Quarterly*. "The Red-Tailed Hawk" appeared in *Dialogue: A Journal of Mormon Thought*.

The Red-Tailed Hawk

I remember how icy the alarm clock was that morning when I jerked it under the covers and fumbled for the button. I didn't want my mother to hear it and get up too, because she would make me eat a cooked breakfast, fix me a big lunch. She would tell me again I shouldn't kill birds, insist how dangerous the river was for me alone, especially in winter, even if I was fifteen, and say that it was almost Christmas. I listened. Then, glad when I couldn't hear her door down the hall, I put the clock back and pulled my Levi's and shirt under the covers to warm. I was going after geese, ducks too, but mostly geese, Canada geese. Standing in the south field after chores, I had seen them twice that week coming up off the lake to feed in the fields. The great grey Canada birds were fantastic, huge almost, wild and free, with a clamorous gabbling that made me shiver. Yet I had never killed one.

"Let me go with you."

I turned to face Glade, the oldest of my three younger brothers, his head just raised off his pillow. How I hated to sleep with him, feel his warmth beside me in the bed, hear him breathe, wake in the night to find him touching me. "No, you can't go. I told you last night."

"I've got some shells. Please, it's Christmas."

"No. Shut up and go back to sleep."

His face pale in the dim light from the frosted windows, he stared at me, then lowered his head and turned to the wall. Glade followed me everywhere, swimming in the summer, fishing, hunting, on hikes. My mother made me let him go, said I should want him to go, that we were brothers. We fought at night. Straddling him I held my pillow over his face, him bucking and twisting, sucking for air; or I jabbed him savagely under the covers until he cried, when my two youngest brothers would holler from their bed that we were fighting. I could hear my father coming. He cuffed me, threatened to lick me, said, "You're not too big yet for a damned good licking." And I hated him for that, for grabbing me by the collar, for kicking me in the butt hard, for always shouting that I was a fool. But I never cried. He couldn't make me.

I wanted to be left alone, wanted that fiercely, didn't want anybody around me, touching me. I wanted to be alone like the birds. Birds were alone. I loved birds. I had taken a taxidermy course, two dollars for each mailed lesson, my haying money, and out in the barn I skinned the birds I killed and made their cotton bodies. I hung them from the barn rafters on long wires, suspended them in flight, meadowlarks, robins, magpies, crows, ducks, hawks, and hanging from the ceiling in my room on a wire, a large red-tailed hawk, wings spread, soaring. Birds could fly wherever they wanted, could be alone. Nothing touched them but the air.

At night, Glade asleep, I would sneak off my pajamas and curl tight under the blankets but not really feel them in the darkness because they were warm like my skin, like air. And that summer often I lay on top of the covers spread out, stared up at the hawk, lifted my naked arms. I fell asleep like that once, and Glade woke before I did.

"You're going to go crazy with that stuff!" my father yelled at me. "What the hell's got into you lately anyway?"

But it wasn't sex, not that kind. I wasn't innocent, for no farm boy could be. But I didn't know girls then, not at fourteen and away from town, and my loins and heart did not burn as they would two years later, although even at fourteen I dreamed and woke in the darkness, my sleep having become frantic with a boy's passion. But mostly I dreamed other dreams, dreams of flying, soaring, lifting away from the earth, being an eagle or a hawk, vanishing into the yellow sun.

My Levi's and shirt got warm under the covers. Feet curled against the cold linoleum, I dressed. Kneeling to feel for my heavy wool boot socks, I looked up at the redtail. "The Albatross—Six-Foot Wingspan," a sailplane I built, had hung there first. Proud of me for once, my father said I should enter it in the county fair. But I didn't. Carrying the five-foot detachable wings, Glade carrying the body because I couldn't carry both, I climbed into the hot summer cliffs, where I sailed it into the afternoon thermals, watched it soar to disappear into the sun. Then I stepped to the very edge, raised my arms. Glade screamed, and he told my father. "You trying to kill yourself, you little fool?" my father yelled at me that night, called me a fool again for losing the plane. Younger, I would let my kites go, hold them until the ten-cent ball of string ended, then let them go, watch the wind carry them.

Careful not to let my drawer squeak, I got my shotgun shells. More than anything else I wanted a room of my own where I could lock the door, be alone, sleep alone, not hear anybody at night, not be touched. And I would have my birds in my room, the soaring hawks and eagles, and the giant grey-white Canada geese. Hanging above my bed on wires, they would be flying, and I could lie there at night looking up at them in the moonlight from the windows or use my flashlight, and perhaps the summer breeze through the open windows would stir them. I would be in a flock of birds.

I remember how I crept down the dark hall, my hand flat against the wall. I closed the hall door and walked through the cold front room past the Christmas tree and into the kitchen. After I ate a bowl of cornflakes I fixed me a sandwich and got my shotgun and other gear. It was two days before Christmas. I hated that too, hated the glittering tree, the music, everybody laughing. But mostly I hated the presents, getting them, people handing me things, putting their arms around me, patting me on the back, wanting something in return. I cringed, wanted to jerk away, run. I wanted the tree down, the ornaments, lights, and Christmas music put away in the cupboard. I wanted the house silent.

I did not dress warm against the cold, although the evening paper had said a big snowstorm was due that afternoon. I wasn't afraid of the cold. I pulled on my hip boots, put my brown canvas hunting coat on over my sweater, fitted my scarf. I didn't build the kitchen fire or turn up the oil heater in the front room. My mother might wake up and, because of the storm, change her mind about me going, or make me take Glade. Through my cotton gloves I felt the cold metal of my shotgun, a double-barrel. I didn't care if they all woke up to a cold house. My father was on graveyard shift at the dairy, but my mother would be up long before he got home a little after eight o'clock.

Closing the back door, I walked down the porch steps, my breath rising in plumes in the icy air. Over the west mountains the moon was a yellow glow behind the clouds. To the east the sky grew white over the mountains. I stopped at the fence at the end of the second field, the crusted snow a foot deep where I stood. My father's small farm was on a bench. Below me were the river bottoms, narrow, then wider where the river neared the lake five miles to the west. Black against the snow, a wide band of cottonwood trees lined the river, a high clump at the swimming hole two miles below the mouth of Spring Creek. In the summer the bottoms were all planted to wheat, oats, sugar beets, and hay, the houses and barns all a mile or two back from the river because of the spring high water. It would be another ten years before they built the dam in the canyon.

I loved that belt of trees and willows, the river. The school, church, my father's house were all alien to me, prisons. I lived my real life there in the bottoms, fished, swam, climbed in the high trees, embraced limbs, sometimes ran naked and alone through the green willows, lay spread-eagle under the sun, soared on the great rope swing, hunted the birds, killed them. I was always hiding from Glade and the others, the sheriff when he came down to see if we wore swimsuits; always driven, I reached out for something infinite, not knowing what it was, but feeling myself drawn to it, some final feeling beyond the earth in the yellow sun.

One set of car lights moved along the bottom road, but I knew I would be the only hunter so late in the season. Those who still hunted had boats and decoys and hunted the open holes on the lake. I climbed between the frosted fence wires and started down the slope. The cattle gathered into the feedlots near the road all day, I would see only the few starved-out horses left in the fields to winter. Sometimes the horses died, froze icy, the legs sticking straight out. When the snow melted, the magpies flocked out of the willows to feed on them.

I would jump shoot Spring Creek to the river and then blind up on a sandbar and wait for the storm to push the geese and big ducks off the lake. Strung out for a mile in the new light, a flock of crows was already coming off the roost. Cawing, black against the snow when they dipped down, a thousand of them maybe, they headed for the cornfields on the bench. Already my hands were cold in the thin gloves, but I shoved only my right hand under my coat. I liked the cold. It was clean and kept people inside. In April and May I swam in the cold river. I liked storms. My mother wanted me home early to help get ready for Christmas, but I would stay late.

I climbed through the last fence and came around a clump of willows. A blue Ford pickup stood parked off the lane near the wooden tractor bridge over Spring Creek. I cursed, the words steady and half silent, like a hiss. A flat sneak boat with two men in it drifted into the first bend as I stepped on the bridge. I watched it vanish into the vapor, the creek just wide enough for it, the voices coming back to me on the water. I cursed them again, loud now, cursed them for the ducks, for being there, for not letting me have it alone, cursed them for their voices and their noise. Then I heard shooting, and I cursed them for that too, even as I loaded my own gun.

I hoped for stragglers out of the small flocks of ducks I saw rise over the willows just ahead of where the boat must have been. But none came. One or two would fall out of the flock; I would hear the dull boom of the shotgun, but no ducks flew close enough for me. I saw no geese. A mile below the tractor bridge, I stopped to warm my hands. Too high for a shot, a magpie flew over me and dropped into a field with a dozen others and some crows near the partially covered skeletons of three cows killed by lightning that summer. Because it was swampy the farmer hadn't been able to drag them out. We had walked the two miles up from the swimming hole to see them the day after. For a month, if the wind was right, you could smell the heavy, watery stink across the fields. What little flesh was left was frozen hard or covered with snow. The magpies and crows watched me pass.

I hunted on down the creek. Magpies were smart. I killed very few of them with my shotgun. I killed them in the early summer with my .22 rifle when, just out of the nest, the young birds couldn't fly far. Tired of swimming, naked, the extra shells brassy in my mouth, I sneaked from tree to tree, shot the young birds, watched them fall in puffs of feather from the high limbs, the screeching old birds too smart to light. Then, because I knew what my mother would say if I brought too many birds home, I tied them with pieces of wire to the fences or climbed to wedge them back in the trees.

The sneak boat was tied up where Spring Creek emptied into the river. The two men sat drinking coffee, the ducks piled on the bow. I crept closer through the willows.

"How about that triple, Fred? Three mallards dead before they hit the water."

I aimed first at him, centering the bead on his head. A little closer, I could have blown big holes in the boat the same way I blew holes in sheds and wooden fences.

"Best shooting I ever saw you do."

I clicked my safety back on, turned and started down the river. Later I heard their motor and knew they had gone back up Spring Creek, knew they had limited out, knew then, too, I was on the river alone.

There was no trail in the snow. I broke my own, cut in and out to the riverbank, but jumped nothing close enough for a shot. Nothing was flying. The wind hadn't really started, wasn't strong enough yet to force the ducks off the lake, keep them low. I stopped often to look for geese against the black mountains and dark clouds, watched until my eyes watered, listened, strained for a sound I could not hear. I knew the storm would bring geese. I'd hunted them since I was twelve and my father let me carry a gun, but I'd never shot one.

I saw small flocks of crows and solitary hawks. Sandbars fed out into the river from the steep banks, but the channel was still full. I had been first across the swimming hole that April, Glade shouting for me to come back, not to try it, that it was too cold, too swift. They'd had to lift me out, build a fire for me. I vomited, blacked out, but I had been first across. I told Glade what I would do to him if he said anything.

I shot a crow that flew over, and it fell into the river. It beat its water-heavy wings and kept lifting its head, but the slow current took it. I liked to touch the birds I killed. A marsh hawk flew by, but not close enough. I watched for the wind in the tops of the trees. Finally, stomping my feet against the numbness, I built a blind on a sandbar where a week earlier I had seen goose tracks and droppings on the edge ice. Warming one hand at a time in my crotch, I ate my lunch and watched the river. A few yellow willow leaves drifted slowly by.

In the summer, alone, my swimming suit hung in a tree, wearing only my Keds, I liked to stand in the willows and let the fluttering green leaves touch me. Rifle in hand, I hunted unseen, alone, sometimes naked except for my feet, shouts drifting to me from the swimming hole. When a thunderstorm came over the west mountains, and the farmers, afraid of being hit by lightning, left the fields, I sneaked out to stand in the belly-high green wheat, watch the great flashes of light, hear the roar and rumble of thunder, feel the wind, the wheat waving against me. Or I climbed high in the bending trees, wrapped my arms and legs around the limbs, squeezed until the rough bark hurt, rode the trees. I loved trees.

And if I tired of hunting birds, I shot the surfacing carp, watched them fade into the deep grey water, set my rifle against a tree, followed them, walked slowly into the river from the sandbars until the water was over my head and the slow summer current carried me. I spread my arms and legs to touch the flesh-warm water, became nothing, only part of the water. Eyes open, I sank down from the grey-blue to the green and then the black, the light disappearing above me, completely alone, touched the cold bottom mud, then rose back again into the light. And I kept doing that until the vomit stung in my throat and I got dizzy. Then I lay in the yellow sun, looked at it through the cracks between my fingers, tried to see what it was. When Glade hollered that he had my clothes, that it was time for chores, I wouldn't answer. Days later I saw the carp near the edge of the water, bleached yellow-white and pecked by magpies.

Small flocks of teal kept flying upriver, but I didn't shoot, didn't want the small ducks. A lone greenhead mallard came up. Watching it through the piled brush, I stood, shot, dropping it dead, ragged, where I could drag it out with a stick, glad it didn't float away out of reach. Sitting in my blind again, I arranged the feathers, stroked them, touched the velvet green head. It was a big northerner with bright orange feet. The winter before on Christmas afternoon I had killed a mallard banded in Alaska. I made a ring out of the aluminum band, which I touched in school, in church, took off, read. Ducks could fly wherever they wanted to, up above everything, just in the air with nothing else around them, never touched by anything except water and air.

It was colder. Blowing across the river from the northeast, the beginning wind scattered a few leaves out of the willows and onto the rippled water. I stomped my feet, rubbed my numb fingers, remembered the story of the hunter who tried to kill his dog, to put his hands in the warm guts to keep them from freezing; but the dog wouldn't come close enough, and the hunter had lost his rifle. Finally I decided to move farther downriver, run part of the way, get warm and blind up again. The wind hit me when I left the willows, and I heard shooting from toward the lake. A few ducks flew against the black clouds; the growing wind would force them down. I heard geese once, pushed back into the willows, saw them off to the south, big, black, five of them, high, their gabbling faint.

I remember how I spoke to them: "Turn, turn," I said, but, heart slamming, had to watch them vanish, just stand there.

I already knew I would stay until dark, knew it before I left the house that morning. I didn't care about my father; maybe he would be asleep, because he had to go on shift at midnight, wouldn't be waiting for me. My mother would just worry, not cuff me, not shout, just look at me, shake her head, talk, her eyes maybe filling up with slow tears, tell me it was Christmastime. The geese would come if I waited long enough. In my mind I saw them, five or six maybe, coming up the river, the great moving wings, necks out, the gabbling louder and louder. And I would kill one, maybe two, bring them crashing down with perfect head shots, the great wings all ragged in the air.

I crossed Spring Creek where a wax sandwich paper from the sneak boat had blown up the creek and caught in the weeds. Three times I cut back in to check the river but jumped nothing, the last time walked through the little grove of six-foot blue spruce. Twice my father had asked me, "Can't you get us a Christmas tree down on the river this year, save me buying one?"

"No," I said, "there aren't any."

"You sure? There used to be a few in the willows if you kept your eyes open."

"No," I said, all the time staring at Glade.

I didn't want to cut a tree, drag it up to the house, hang it with tinsel and lights, didn't want the smell of it in the house away from the river, didn't want to watch it turn brown. A hundred yards back from the spruces, under the snow, were the bones of a little spike buck I had killed a year earlier in August. He had followed the river out of the canyon. I shot him through the eye with my .22, watched him until he was quiet, and then turned him over so he didn't look hurt. I went back three times that day, squatted down by him, brushed off the ants. The second day the magpies were on him.

Except for a few horse tracks, the snow was clean, and I broke my own trail. Way ahead where the river curved, I saw the high cottonwoods at the swimming hole. It took five boys just to reach around the biggest tree, the rope tree. It was an old rope, two inches thick and frayed. We had board platforms nailed in the trees to swing from, but I liked to climb higher, up into the green leaves. The others watched me, faces upturned, Glade shouting for me not to go any higher, maybe bawling. Sometimes, standing on a limb, I let go and stood on just one foot to have the feeling, then grabbed the overhead branch again when I tipped. I liked the feeling, the shiver.

Holding the rope, chest tight, I lifted up, and it was like in my dreams when I flew over houses and trees with just my arms outspread. The warm air rushing against me, the trees blurred, I waited until just before I hit the top of the sweep before I let go. And for that one moment I flew, saw everything below me, soared, hovered. Then I dropped, felt the tingling in my crotch, felt the air, the rushing, heavier water. And I stayed under until they all thought I had drowned. I was both bird and fish. If anybody climbed as high as I had, I would climb higher, swinging again and again, falling until my nose bled, and I let the blood fall on my naked chest and stomach so that I looked wounded. The letting go, the soaring, was the very best part. I wanted to feel like that forever.

I built another blind on a sandbar above the swimming hole. The wind made the cold worse. I couldn't see my breath anymore. I kept my hands under my armpits, stomped my feet on the packed snow. Walking home I would be facing into the wind all the way. I knew that it was nearly four o'clock, that I should have been at least back to the tractor bridge on Spring Creek. People would be turning on their outside Christmas lights. The steady shooting from toward the lake meant more birds were flying. Teal kept slipping up the river in easy range, but I didn't shoot. I dropped a hen mallard out of a flock of five on the second shot. She was easy to reach. She was big, an orange-footed northerner, and I decided I would mount her too, when I did the goose, put her near a big greenhead I had hanging in the barn, make a pair. I liked the wind. I liked to go out in the barn on windy days, leave the door open and watch the birds move.

Later I climbed the bank to look for geese. Under the low, heavy clouds everything was almost black, even the snow. Willows clicked. Lower now, the ducks came in against the wind in singles and doubles and small flocks. Dipping down, wings whistling when they flew over, they came on, the wind forcing them lower. I saw two small flocks of geese, strained to hear them above the wind, stared them out of sight, hoping all the time they would turn, come my way, talked to them. But they kept on, drawn to some other place, left me empty.

Below the geese white points of light burned in the houses along the bench, the outside Christmas lights not visible from that distance. My mother would be pushing back the curtain at the kitchen window to look out. But I didn't care. In front of me, black against the grey snow, stood a starved-out old horse, head down, tail to the wind. Beyond the horse, only a black dot, was the big haystack at the end of Miller's Lane. The horse was the only thing in the fields I could see alive. Swaying the tops of the trees, the wind brought the first scattered flakes of snow.

Just after I got back in my blind, two big greenhead mallards flew by in easy range, but I didn't shoot. More big ducks came. But I was waiting for geese, only geese. They liked to rest in the shallows along the sandbars, leave their sign. But they came late, and I, afraid of my father, had never dared stay. They would come though, I knew, if only I waited long enough. I listened against the wind, strained my watery eyes to watch down the river, watched, stomped my feet only when I couldn't stand the numbness, pounded my gloved hands against my knees, sure the geese would come, absolutely sure.

The big haystack at the end of Miller's Lane was where we left our bicycles when we went down to swim. August had been very hot, and I remember one night how I got up, dressed and climbed out the bedroom window. I intended only to ride my bicycle up and down the road in front of the house to get cool, but I turned off on the bottom road and then onto Miller's Lane, parked my bicycle. At first I took off only my shirt, but then my Keds and socks, and then, carrying my clothes, I was running naked down the sandy path, leaping, watching my legs flash in the moonlight. I wanted to scream and yell, throw my clothes away, run through the fields of ripe August wheat, but I didn't because I knew a farmer might be out with a late water turn, or I might cut my feet. The cows and horses did not shy as I ran past them.

The cottonwood trees shaded the moonlight from the swimming hole. The dark air over me, I floated, tried not to move, the water fusing with the darkness. When I climbed the trees the dark leaves touched me. The second night, in a wind I rode the trees, the high limbs, heard a million leaves, screamed into the sound. And when I swung on the rope it was fantastic because I couldn't see where the water started. The tingling went from my crotch clear to my skull, and I reached out to a world I had never known, something inviting me, as in my dreams.

I left the house four times at night, until on the fourth morning at three o'clock, my father was waiting for me in the yard. "What the hell you doing out at this hour?" he said, spun me around, felt my damp hair. "You young fool, you trying to commit suicide down there swimming alone at night?'' I didn't answer. He backhanded me, told me what it was like to drown, shouted, said he'd beat me next time. I had to stay on the place for a week. "Fool," he said. "I'll send the sheriff after you if you try it again." At breakfast Glade kept snickering.

More ducks flew up the river, flocks. I knew it would soon be dark. And then I heard them, that gabbling, the sound at first like the wind. I listened, already reaching for my shotgun, as if by instinct I knew the sound was geese. They were on the river. My breath caught. Heavy loads already chambered, I crouched on the snow, pushed the safety off, smothered the sound with my glove, tightened my legs. Low, gabbling, three great Canada geese flew out of the greyness below me, shadows, but then blacker, coming right at me in good range. Big, bigger than I had ever thought, beautiful, somebody pounding me over the heart. I watched through a hole in the blind. "Wait, wait," whispering, "not too soon, not too soon. Big. Wait, wait." The gabbling grew louder—marvelous the wings, the long necks, the rhythmic birds.

Just as they came abreast I stood up. Flaring, they lifted with the wind, moving away. I shot, missed, shot again, and the lead goose turned completely over and fell broken-winged, crashing into the water. Even as he hit I was out of the blind, mindless of the other geese, ready to dance and scream. Upright, trailing the wing, the goose swam toward the far side. Cramming in a shell, I aimed carefully at the head and fired. The long neck collapsed, and the head pushed forward into the water under the force of the shot. The pounding in my chest died. The wind and the slow current moved him. He was too far out.

I didn't hesitate. I set my gun on my coat. When I pulled off my Levi's the cold wind stung my bare legs. Puffs of mud rose around my feet when I stepped into the river past the edge ice, the water colder than the wind.

I swam sidestroke, the goose bobbing ahead of me on the waves I made. I wasn't afraid, though I knew I could cramp, sink, fade down into the grey water and yellow leaves. It didn't seem strange, not unreal, not dangerous. I reached out and took the goose by the neck, glad, wanting to shout, the feathers warm. And then, not feeling my body under the water, frozen, I turned back. When I touched the mud under me, I stumbled out and dropped the goose. Yellow, the broken wingbone stuck out through the feathers. I picked up the goose again and hugged it to me, felt the still-warm body against my numb skin.

The wind had blown my shirt and left glove into the water. My body was white. My head buzzed. I kept gasping for breath, and acid vomit rose in my throat as I tried to dry myself with my undershirt. When I tried to pull on my Levi's, I stumbled, covering my feet with the white snow. Dressed, I put the stiffening wet glove, shirt, and undershirt into the rear game pocket with the ducks, picked up the heavy goose, my shotgun, and struggled up the bank. The wind hit me square, blew the snow hard into my eyes, took my breath.

After ten minutes, fumbling, I stopped to brush the snow off my coat and to wrap my scarf around my face. Still my face slowly stiffened, and it was hard to open my mouth. My forehead ached; the snow filled my eyes. I carried the goose over my shoulder; my bare left hand had become wood or stone. Everything was black, even the sky, the only light coming from the grey snow under me. I couldn't see Spring Creek or the river. At first when I stumbled, the snow was colder than the wind, but only at first. The cold was like pressing naked against ice. I kept trying to brush the snow off my coat so I wouldn't be white. A magpie rose screeching from a willow clump and was whipped away by the wind. My shotgun was gone.

I pushed on and on against the wind and driving snow until I could not feel myself walking. I kept stumbling and falling. I wasn't carrying the Canada goose over my shoulder. I didn't know where I was. I seemed not even to breathe. I floated, left the ground, rose, hovered, and it was a sensation I had never known before. I expected to see the fences, willows, and trees vanish under me. I was becoming something beyond myself. I felt no limits, nothing stopping, nothing touching me, as if I were rising alone into light, rising, never falling back, the sensation never ending.

I stumbled a last time, fell forward into the soft snow, where I lay on my side not caring, the snow not cold anymore. Relaxed, sleepy almost, I stared at the white snow falling on my coat, saw then the horn and half-head of one of the summer lightning-killed cows. I raised my head, saw behind me the mound I had stumbled over. I crawled. Mechanically with my lower arms and dead hands, I pushed back the snow from the horn, saw the black, empty eye socket, the bone skull. I looked down. Snow filled the wrinkles of my coat; I was turning white.

All summer the cows had been vanishing, the wire-hung birds too, the carp, the little buck. And I had no name for it, only vanishing, knew only that it was not swimming, not running naked in the moonlight, not embracing trees, not soaring. It was not feeling. I grew whiter, saw myself vanishing into the snow. I watched, and then slowly, like beginning pain, the terror seeped into me, the knowing. I struggled up, fled.

But I could not run, could not feel the ground through my feet to balance myself. When I fell I got up, pushed with my elbows, feeling no pain, my hands and feet gone. I found low places in the fences and fell forward, the wire tearing my clothes. I thought the posts and bushes were people rushing up to help me.

I could only see, not smell, hear, even my tongue cold in my mouth. And I wanted to raise my arms around my head to keep it warm so I could go on seeing, for I was afraid my eyes would freeze and I would fall down and be covered by the snow. But I couldn't raise my arms.

And then I stopped, stood.

A light flashed through the driving snow. It was red. It flashed again. I saw headlights, and I began to run. I stumbled and I got up. I climbed up a bank. I fell down on my hands and knees. I looked at tire tracks filling with snow. I was on the lane. Slowly I stood up. I waited.

The headlights turned and came dipping, vanishing, a spotlight sweeping ahead and to the sides through the driving snow. The spotlight hit me and didn't move. The car came ahead and stopped, the red light on top flashing. It was the sheriff's car. The sheriff got out. He pulled his broad-brimmed hat tight against the wind. He buttoned the collar of his heavy coat. He stopped in front of me. He asked me my name. I stared at him. "Hell, kid, you've got your mother all upset. Your old man's out searching the fields with half-a-dozen neighbors in this storm. He's mad too, I can tell you that. You could freeze to death in no time out here with the wind blowing this hard."

The sheriff blocked out the lights.

Again he asked me my name. "What's wrong with you, kid, can't you talk?" He played his flashlight up and down me. "Where's your gun?" He stepped closer. "Where's your glove?" He shined the light into my eyes, and I couldn't close them. "Good hell, kid, we better get you in where it's warm." I felt him take my arm, grip it tight, and I fell toward his hand.

I was in the hospital three weeks. The surgeon cut three fingers on my left hand off down to the first knuckle, and afterward my hand was a white ball raised on a wire frame. I had pneumonia. The oxygen tent was like being underwater. When I rose up out of the blackness, I saw my mother or my father, sometimes both. My father sat in a chair and slept with his forehead resting on my bed. Then I would sink back down into the blackness again, spiral down into the not-knowing, vanish.

I was terrified of sleep. When I was out of the oxygen tent and could talk again, I told the doctor my hand didn't hurt so he would stop the shots for pain. At first he said no, but later he told the nurse. The pain wouldn't let me sleep too long. I cried sometimes at night because of the pain, but it was better than sleep.

Across from me was an old man with yellow skin who slept all of the time. At night I listened to him breathe, his mouth a black hole in the dim light. They kept putting his thin yellow arms and legs back under the covers. The nurses hurried to put a screen around my bed the night he died, but through the cracks I saw what they did. Later, after the nurse took the screen away, I watched two women turn over the mattress and put on all fresh bedding. They whispered back and forth across the bed and looked at me. A nurse made me take a sleeping pill.

When the doctor released me my father wrapped me in a blanket and carried me from the hospital door to the car in his arms, the corner of the blanket over my face. It was late afternoon when we got home. The whole family came out as we pulled in. My brothers were dressed in their Sunday clothes; my mother wiped her eyes with the bottom edge of her blue apron. My father carried me into the warm house that smelled of roast turkey and put me on the couch in the front room. Blazing in the corner was the Christmas tree with everybody's presents under it. They had saved Christmas for me, which I hadn't known. I bit my lip and turned away. Glade wanted to know what was wrong. "Nothing," I said.

Several neighbors came by to bring me presents; then we had supper, and after that, Christmas. My little brothers brought me my presents, helped me with the ribbons, stacked my presents for me. Later my mother said that I'd had enough excitement and needed to rest, so my father carried me down the hall to the bedroom. The bedroom was warm from a new oil heater. Warm under the covers in my heavy flannel pajamas, I lay and listened to my brothers playing in the front room. Above me the red-tailed hawk still hovered, the tail fanned, the wings spread to hold the air, the beak wide for screaming. The yellow glass eyes looked down, the bird motionless, dusty, suspended from a wire. Out in the barn the hanging birds were dusty too, some of them splotched with pigeon droppings.

That night Glade was supposed to sleep on the couch in the front room, where I could be during the day, but I didn't want him to. I told my mother he wouldn't hurt my hand, so she let him sleep with me. Later, just before he went on graveyard shift, my father came and stood in the doorway, the hall light behind him. He could see I was still awake, everybody else asleep.

"You all right, son?" he asked, quietly.

"I guess so," I said.

That was all he said. He stood there for a moment; then, leaving the door half open, turned and walked down the hall. He didn't turn the hall light off.

My presents were stacked on the dresser in front of the mirror. Over the sound of the heater I heard the wind outside. It was snowing. I raised my arm to turn the white ball of my hand in the light from the hall. I hadn't seen my hand yet. When I did, I cried like a baby in the doctor's office. At school I kept my hand hidden in my pocket, wore the same sweater every day because it had front pockets, and I stopped going to gym. I couldn't stand being dressed in a gym uniform, my arms bare; couldn't stand it in the showers naked, without even a towel to cover my hand; couldn't stand the other boys seeing me. Clutching my hand I prayed at night, even out loud, promised God everything, then woke in the early morning afraid to look. But my father made me start gym again.

"You can't hide; you have to live with it," he said.

And he made me do my chores, no matter how hard, no matter how many things I broke or spilled; and although he shouted at me sometimes, swore, he never again hit me.

Green, blue, white, red—the colored Christmas boxes and wrappings glinted on the dresser in the shaft of light from the half-open door. I stared up at the hawk. It was indistinct now, black, a hovering silhouette, a dark, still shadow above me. I moved closer to Glade, touched him. The dresser mirror reflected the boxes and packages. I had received the most presents.

THE GOLD MINE

Standing at the kitchen sink looking out the window, Mrs. Miller watched the truck come out of the dark mouth of the canyon, the long plume of dust spreading slowly out over the sagebrush and rocks on both sides. The windshield flashed the late-afternoon desert sun.

"Now, I wonder what he's back down here for so soon." She looked at the big watch on her wrist and then up at the clock on the yellow wall. She stood on her toes to see above the potted red geraniums between the yellow curtains.

Mrs. Miller's three dogs ran out as the small yellow pickup turned off and came up her lane to the heavy trees shading the house, and stopped by the lamppost. The dust spread out over the small lawn and border of flowers.

"Well," she said. Reaching over to turn down her radio on the counter, she moved from the kitchen window. Her two cats followed her into the front room. The two parakeets called in unison as she left. She opened the front door and pushed open the storm door, the swamp-cooler air rushing out around her. She looked down at Carl, who stood at the bottom of the porch steps.

"What's wrong, Carl? I can tell by your face something is wrong."

"He's dead."

"Who's dead?" Mrs. Miller walked out on the covered porch. "Who's dead?"

"The boy."

"The boy? Richard?" Carl nodded his head.

"Richard? I just saw him not three hours ago on that red dirt bike of his. Dead? How is he dead? Killed in that old mine shaft, I wouldn't wonder. Looking for gold?"

Carl nodded.

"Dead. Who would believe it? I just saw him not . . . the poor darling, the poor darling." She wiped the tears from her eyes with her apron. "Oh, Carl, come in, come in. Don't just stand there in that heat. Come in the house where it's cool. You'll die of sunstroke. Stomp the dust off your feet. Come on, Carl. You need help. In this ol' world you're alive one minute and dead the next."

Mrs. Miller turned and held the storm door open, her right arm held out to Carl, who came slowly up the steps, across the porch, and into the front room. Mrs. Miller closed the door behind her. She took Carl by the hand.

"Richard, Richard." With her free hand Mrs. Miller wiped her eyes with her apron. "This desert's no place for a boy or any other human being, either, who's got any sense. It's been forty years, but I still dream about my Billy."

Letting go of Carl's hand, Mrs. Miller turned and took from among the gold-framed pictures on top of the piano the picture of a smiling boy. She wiped her eyes again. "Have I ever showed you Billy's picture, Carl? Pneumonia took him." She looked at Carl. "Of course I haven't showed you. You've never been in this house in the two years you've been living up there taking care of that old mine, though you've been invited often enough to come to supper and watch a little TV and enjoy life a little."

Mrs. Miller put the picture in Carl's hand for him to look at, and then she took it again. She kissed the boy's face and put the picture back. "He was a wonderful son. And there's his father Joe, and Max and Fred." Mrs. Miller pointed to the three other large pictures on the piano among the smaller pictures. "I've buried three good husbands. A woman couldn't ask for more than that. They're all waiting for me now." She held up her hand. "This is Fred's watch I'm wearing. He always said I was hard on watches. You got to keep track of time."

She turned from the pictures to look at Carl.

"You don't have any pictures in that old cabin. You ought to have pictures of pretty girls, a young man like you. Mae and me drove up a dozen times to leave you something nice to eat, but you're never there. Mel tells me you don't buy nothing at the store now except canned beans. What kind of food's that to enjoy? You're as thin as a rail. You haven't shaved for a month, and you need a good bath and clean clothes. Next you'll forget how to talk. I've seen it all before. There's old worthless mines in all these canyons along the valley."

Mrs. Miller wiped her eyes and cheeks again.

"What will Richard's mother do? She'll never forgive herself for letting him come out to this desert. All the rest of her life she'll want to hold him again. Don't I know. It doesn't matter how many kids you got either. But nobody's to blame. These things happen to us all. That's life. I thank the good Lord every day on my knees for two daughters and nine grandchildren. I've got high blood pressure and diabetes myself, so you never know. We've all got something."

Mrs. Miller walked to the front window and pushed the pink curtain further back to look up toward the canyon. She shook her head. As she turned she reached down to pick a dead leaf off one of the potted geraniums on the windowsill.

"Poor boy." She looked at the grandfather clock stand-ing in the corner by the door and shook her head. "Dead, and I saw him alive at noon. Funny. He came right to the mouth of the canyon a few minutes behind you, but he turned on that red dirt bike of his and went back up the road after he saw you make the turn toward the junction. I've seen him do that before. Up to some devilment, most likely, while you were gone." Wiping her cheeks and eyes, she turned back to Carl. "Was Richard smashed up bad, Carl? I'll help you lay him out."

Mrs. Miller looked at Carl.

"What?"

"Oh, you'll have to wash the poor darling and dress him in clean clothes. Nobody else to do that but you and me out in the middle of this desert. You might have to build a box for him too, depending on how far you have to take him. It'll have to be deep to hold ice. I'll help you take care of him. I've done it often enough, and my mother and grandmother before me."

Mrs. Miller smoothed her apron with both hands.

"Come in the kitchen and sit down for a minute and catch your breath before you call the sheriff, Carl. You look like you need it. I made a cake this morning, and I just finished baking bread. It's a good job done. Go on." She shook her head. "And we all thought Richard would be such nice company for you."

Mrs. Miller walked behind Carl into the kitchen.

"Sit down there at the table." Mrs. Miller sat down in a large rocking chair between the table and the stove. Both cats jumped into her lap. "The sheriff can wait a minute. You look all tired out. You're so thin. Your bones will soon be poking through your skin. It must have been quite a shock for you if you're not used to finding dead bod-ies. Used to be a little cemetery up at the mine, but it got washed out thirty years ago in a big cloudburst. We had bones scattered all down the canyon." Mrs. Miller shook her head. "Poor souls. Sit down." Mrs. Miller nodded at the table. Carl sat down. "You're glad to be able to sit down as you get older, I can tell you that."

Mrs. Miller stroked the two cats.

"It's nobody's fault. Don't start feeling responsible for Richard's death now. Why, his father sat right in that chair when he brought him out here from Utah two weeks ago and told me he wanted him to run loose." Carl looked at the chair Mrs. Miller nodded toward. "He stopped for directions to the mine. He said he couldn't do anything with him anymore. He just wanted Richard to ride that dirt bike of his across this desert till he got some of the hell out of his system. He'd decided he couldn't keep Richard from breaking his neck if that's what he wanted to do. Owning stock in that worthless gold mine, I guess he figured he would get something out of it, as long as you were here to keep an eye on his boy. People buy stock in these old mines expecting whole veins of new gold to be found, but they never will. All three of my husbands had stock given to them, but they weren't fools enough to think it would be worth anything. Fred had a cousin killed at the old Black Canyon Mine. He fell into a ball mill and got crushed to powder along with the ore. They just emptied the bin into a truck and buried that. People from all over the county came to the funeral. It took two men with shovels three days to dig a grave big enough. We didn't have backhoes much in those days."

Mrs. Miller shook her head; she stroked both cats.

"Richard's father said he'd pay for all damages even before he left. Richard stole one of my hens the first week he was here. I saw him sneaking off with it. Cooked it over a fire up that canyon, I guess. Why, just Tuesday he burned down one of the Campbells' old lambing sheds. Mae saw him riding away on that red bike, even if it was dark. She called me right after, and I saw him go racing past here on the road like the devil himself was after him.

He must have bought a gunnysack full of those big fire-crackers Mel has at the junction. You hear them going off day and night. Itha and Cosette seen him go racing by their places at night on that bike naked as the day he was born, except for a pair of shorts, and without shoes even."

Mrs. Miller set the cats on the floor and stood up.

"Well, you'd better call Sheriff Wilson, Carl. You can get Sid through the highway patrol dispatcher. After that you need to call Richard's father. That'll be hard, but it's something you have to do. I've made that kind of call often enough out in this desert in the last fifty years."

Mrs. Miller put her hand on Carl's arm.

"I expect we'll have to take Richard as far as the junction at least, and maybe farther. Why, Fred and I took a body all the way to Los Angeles once twenty years ago, just before he got sick. We had to stop for ice three times. My, but people were curious when we did that. Sid will give you a death certificate and a permit to transport the body. He carries the books right with him. He's deputy county coroner. All these sheriffs have to be, out in this desert. Come on, Carl. It's your job to do."

Carl stood up, and Mrs. Miller followed him to the phone on the wall. She showed him the highway patrol number written on the calendar. Carl dialed the number. Standing by his side, Mrs. Miller reached up and pulled his hand down so the receiver was tipped away from his ear.

The dispatcher radioed the sheriff, who was ten miles north of the junction investigating the deaths of two tourists whose Jeep had rolled down a mountain. The dispatcher said it would take him an hour to get to the ranch.

"Sorry to hear about your accident, Carl. Let us know if we can be of any more help. That's tough on everybody for a boy that young to get killed. Let us know. Tell Maude hello."

"I'm right here, Boyd."

"Well, good to hear your voice, Maude. Too bad about that boy. A real shame. We'll all miss him."

"Yes, it is. He was a fine boy. You don't like to see young people going before their time."

"Well, got another call, Maude. Sounds like some tourists got lost out toward Iron Springs. Let us know if we can help you any."

"Thanks, Boyd." Carl hung up the receiver. "Boyd's been dispatcher for twenty years."

She turned to look at Carl.

"Now, call Richard's father. The number's right there on the wall in red. It's Saturday, so he ought to be home. He left the number in case of an emergency. Go on."

Carl dialed.

"Tell him, Carl."

"Dead?" the father said. "Dead? My boy dead?"

The father left the phone and then returned. "I'll call you back. You've been very kind." The click of his phone cut off the sound of a woman screaming.

Mrs. Miller reached up and took the receiver from Carl and hung it up. "Poor dears. News like that is always a real shock, even if you're expecting it. Oh, the calls I've had to make. We should have left this desert to the lizards and vultures long ago." Mrs. Miller shook her head. "I hope Richard has brothers and sisters."

Mrs. Miller walked over to the refrigerator and opened it. She looked at her watch and then at the alarm clock on the counter. "Now, you sit down and I'll fix you a sandwich out of this new bread while we're waiting for Sid and his deputy."

Bending down, she poured milk for the cats and put the plastic gallon bottle on the counter.

"No."

"Yes, you're going to have something. Now don't tell me any different. You're not getting out of this house without eating something. We all need to keep our strength up at a time like this. I know what I'm talking about. I've got this bread fresh out of the oven. Now you sit back down at that table and have a nice sandwich and a glass of cold milk. It'll do you good."

Mrs. Miller pointed to the chair with the long, thin bread knife. Carl sat down. She spread the new bread with thick butter, then mayonnaise. She cut slices of cheese, tomato, and roast beef to lay on the lettuce. She put the heavy sandwich down in front of Carl on a white plate and poured milk into a tall, clear glass.

"Now eat that and enjoy it."

Mrs. Miller sat back down in her rocking chair. "Oh, that cooler is nice out in this desert. Joe put that in for me the year before he died."

Carl ate slowly, blinking his eyes.

"Why, I can see every bite going down, Carl. You're nothing but skin over bones. You'll die and won't even know it. That sun will bloat you up just like a dead sheep. How do you expect to live on canned beans and stay healthy? I've told Mel to have you stop by and get a loaf of homemade bread or an apple pie I baked and froze for you, but you never have. Mae and me invited you to our Thanksgiving and Christmas dinners both years. You didn't come, though. If I could drive, I'd have been up that canyon after you. You've never come to any of our parties or to church at the junction. We like to be friendly around here. You ought to have you a dog up there to keep you company, if you can't get a pretty little wife right now. You're only young once."

Carl ate slowly, his eyes wide open. "You want another one, Carl?" He shook his head. "There's plenty here; you can have two more if you want." Still chewing, he shook his head. "Mel says you never get any letters and nobody ever comes to visit."

Mrs. Miller stood up and walked to the counter past the two cats finishing up the milk in the bowl.

"How about a piece of this chocolate cake then, and a big scoop of vanilla ice cream?" She set the chocolate cake down in front of Carl on the table and lifted the clear plastic top from the cake saver. "My, don't that smell good? Wish I could have a big piece with ice cream, but I don't dare. My diabetes has been acting up a little lately. I have it for folks who drop by."

He shook his head.

"You sure, Carl? Chocolate was my Fred's favorite. How about some cookies and milk, or maybe some nice chocolates? I always keep a box in the fridge. Max and Joe both liked chocolates."

He shook his head.

"Well, maybe you'll want a piece when Sid and his deputy get here. Sid likes chocolate cake. I've known Sid for over thirty years."

Mrs. Miller put the top back on the cake saver and sat down in her rocking chair. Looking out the big kitchen window toward the shadowed dark mouth of the canyon, she shook her head.

"That handsome boy, but at least he isn't out there in the desert puffing up like a dead sheep, with the ravens and vultures working on him already. In this heat it only takes an hour." The cats had jumped back into her lap, and she stroked them with both hands. "Sometimes the only thing to do is use one of those zip-up plastic bags the morticians give me. You learn to stay upwind too, I'll tell you that, if there is any wind. Of course, winter's bad too. The Clarks had a sheepherder who went through the ice on his horse and then tried to ride back in a blizzard and froze. The horse brought him back to the barn all right, but he was frozen so solid we couldn't even get the reins out of his hands. Of course, he'd wrapped them around his hands and kept hold of the saddle horn when he could see he wasn't going to make it. We finally had to take him and the bridle and the saddle in the kitchen to thaw him loose. We had an awful mess, I'll tell you that. Sheepherders are funny."

Mrs. Miller shook her head and looked back from the window at Carl.

"Fred always was a great help in a case like that. He made a fine box, and he could dig a nice grave too, if it was needed. He never charged anybody a dime. We all have to do what we can. I'd help him build the box, and he'd help me do the laying out. I didn't do much digging though. Poor Fred, to die like he did, all that suffering. Cancer of the liver. He was a good husband to me for thirty years. Before that I had Joe for almost ten. Joe went quick, a heart attack. That's the way to go if you have to go. Max died of diabetes just like I've got. I only had him for five years. Billy was gone in three days. Now him and those three good men are all waiting for me. What would we do without the good Lord to help us along the way?"

The phone rang.

"Well, I wonder who that is." She looked at her watch and up at the wall clock.

The cats jumped to the floor as Mrs. Miller stood up to answer the phone. Holding her hand over the receiver, she spoke to Carl at the table. "It's Mae. She just saw the sheriff drive by her place and wondered if I knew what he was out this way for." Mrs. Miller took her hand off the receiver. "I was just going to call you, Mae. We've had a bad accident."

She explained to Mae about Richard.

"I don't know for sure yet. But it'll be after dark. You watch for us. I'll have Carl blink his lights. We'll have to take Richard as far as the junction anyway. They never come off the freeway with those big Cadillac hearses. You call Cosette and Itha, will you, and tell them?"

Through the big window she watched Sheriff Wilson drive up the lane, the dogs and dust following him.

"Sid just got here, Mae. We'll blink our lights. Let everybody know. How you feeling today? Better? Good." She hung up and turned to Carl. "Just us old folks on these little ranches now. Kids leave as soon as they're old enough. Of course, ranchin' on this desert never did pay much."

After Sheriff Wilson took statements from both Mrs. Miller and Carl, Mrs. Miller got cake and milk for him and his deputy. She put a big scoop of ice cream on each piece of cake. "Sure you don't want a piece, Carl?"

He shook his head.

"I got some day-old apple pie here, Sid, if you'd like a piece. It's not fresh, but it's still pretty good. Mae was over yesterday."

"Sure, pile it on, Maude."

The deputy nodded his head. "Good."

"Just so you enjoy it; that's what it's for."

The phone rang. It was Richard's uncle. The sheriff stood up and took the receiver from Mrs. Miller.

"Yes. Yes," he said. He nodded his head. He put his hand over the receiver and turned to Carl.

"They want to know if you'll take Richard across the Utah border to Nephi and meet the family and the hearse from Provo there. It's the quickest way. Those hearses ain't refrigerated, and they can't break one loose anyway to come three hundred miles until late tomorrow. He'll keep better anyway in the back of your pickup on ice in a box. Maude here will help you. You'll do that won't you, Maude?"

"Be real happy to."

"Bert and me will help you on the box. We probably got a little while before we get another call. The boy's mother's gone all to pieces, and his dad isn't much better. They've still got the doctor with her."

"Of course he'll go, Sid, won't you, Carl? I'll go with you." From her rocking chair, Mrs. Miller looked across the table at Carl. "We all have to help out, Carl, at a time like this."

Carl looked at Mrs. Miller.

"Thanks, Carl." Sheriff Wilson turned back to the wall phone. "Okay, Mr. Nelson, Carl will be more than happy to do it. Mrs. Miller will be coming too. Let me write that down. Sorry, Mr. Nelson. Once more? Got it. We're awfully sorry about Richard. He must have been a real fine boy. It's too bad." The sheriff looked at his watch. "I'll call you back after we've been up to the mine. Sure sorry. Good-bye."

The sheriff hung up and turned to Carl, who sat at the table looking at his hands. "Here, you better take this, Maude, so you'll know where to meet the hearse in Nephi."

"Well, we better get a move on," Mrs. Miller said, taking the slip of paper. "I've got my suitcase all ready right here in the closet. Here, Bert, you cut you and Sheriff Wilson another piece of cake." She stood up from the rocking chair. "I want each of you to take a loaf of this new bread home with you too. There's sacks in the top drawer."

The sheriff held out his plate for his second piece of cake. "You ought to try this, Carl." The sheriff took the piece of cake from the plate with his fingers. "This is the only way to eat chocolate cake. Good, Carl." The deputy took his slice of cake in his hand.

The sheriff took a bite of the cake.

"Don't you worry about a thing, Carl. Mel's always got plenty of ice on hand at the junction. He don't have much business since the freeway went through. Mostly local people." The sheriff took another big bite of cake. "Bert and me will help you till we have to go, and nobody knows more about laying them out than Maude here does. Do they, Maude?"

"Don't think so, Sid, but then I've had years of experience."

"Old folks in the county make arrangements with Maude beforehand, or they leave a note if they have time. I guess they like to have that much done by somebody they know before one of those city morticians gets ahold of them. Don't they, Maude?"

"Yes."

Mrs. Miller stood at the sink spooning liquid from a small brown bottle into a white plastic gallon bottle. A large black suitcase lay open on the counter.

"Maude here's seen it all, Carl. She's lived in this damned desert all her life. Nobody knows what keeps her going, but she still gets a kick out of life. She had a stroke two years ago. Didn't you, Maude?"

The deputy put the two loaves of bread in the brown paper sacks and laid them on the table. The sheriff licked the rest of the chocolate from his fingers and then wiped them with his white paper napkin. He looked at his watch.

"You planning on spending another winter up here, Carl?"

Carl looked at his hands on the table. "Yes."

"Some of us were hoping you might have decided to go to college or someplace where there's girls. Living alone too long in that cabin up at that mine, you want to be careful. Quite a few young fellows your age get jobs babysitting these old gold mines, but this desert ain't no place to try to live without friends and family, I can tell you that."

The sheriff wet the end of his forefinger with his tongue and picked up a crumb of cake from his plate and put it into his mouth.

"Ain't that right, Bert?"

"That's right."

"Why, I've seen men go completely nuts after a year or two of living alone up one of these canyons. They stop eatin' any decent food, and then they stop talking. After that they hide back in these old mine shafts, only coming out at night like owls. We had one young fellow up Troy Canyon staying in an old cabin just like you. Used to sit on a ledge all curled up out in that sun for hours naked as a jaybird. Looked like he never did take a bath, the dust on him in layers. Had a beard two feet long, if it was an inch. We finally had to go after him with a net, didn't we, Bert? Took six men. I thought we'd have to use a dart gun on him. Why, they start hugging trees and listening to rocks. They talk to squirrels and magpies. But it's when they start making pets out of Gila monsters and rattlesnakes, they find out this desert ain't the Garden of Eden. There was only one of those, and it didn't last long. Richard must have been company for you, Carl."

"Well, I'm all ready, Sid." Mrs. Miller stood at the sink screwing the lid on the plastic gallon bottle. "I just had to mix up some of this fresh. I don't know when I'll get a call, so I've always got things pretty well ready."

The sheriff stood up. "Take that suitcase, Bert."

"Now don't you two forget your bread, whatever you do. Thank you, Bert. I'll carry the bottle."

"My wife's going to give me a big kiss when I bring home a loaf of Maude's bread, Bert. She sure enjoys it. What'll your wife give you?"

Everybody laughed but Carl.

"How's Jane feeling since her operation, Sid?" Mrs. Miller dried her hands on a towel.

"Good. Good."

"How are all the kids?"

"Good. Only one left home now."

Mrs. Miller shook her head. "Well we better get a move on." She looked at her two clocks. "We've got to build a nice deep box and get Richard laid out. It'll work out about right. We don't want to bring him down until after it starts to cool off a little. But we don't want to be late meeting those folks in Nephi. You ought to wear a watch, Carl."

Mrs. Miller turned up the kitchen radio and switched on a lamp in the front room. She said good-bye to her cats and parakeets. She sprinkled food in the fish tank. She reached down and petted the two cats. "Now, you two be good while I'm gone. Come on, Carl."

Outside, Mrs. Miller had Carl load Fred's toolbox into the back of the pickup.

"What's wrong with this tailgate, Carl?" The tailgate lay flat. She tried to raise it. She set the plastic bottle down on the truck bed and took a hammer from the toolbox. "This hinge is bent." She hit the hinge with the hammer to straighten it, and then oiled it with the can from the toolbox. "Now try it." Carl raised the tailgate and it locked in place. "There," she said.

"Maude's great at fixing things, Carl. These Jap pickups are kind of small ain't they?"

Carl and Bert loaded the lumber from the shed at the side of the house and tied it down.

"Fred always bought number-one pine, so I always keep some on hand. He said it was the least we could do. But he never charged anybody a dime. That's the kind of man he was. Said we all had to help when people were in trouble." She walked over to the twenty-foot-high lamppost and pushed the switch. "Might as well turn that on now. It'll be dark by the time we get back." Bending down a little, she petted the dogs. "Now, you boys stay here."

The sheriff had Bert drive Carl's small pickup so Carl could ride with him and Mrs. Miller up the canyon.

"You sit in the middle, Carl." Mrs. Miller pushed the plastic bottle down between them. "That's not too tight, is it?" Carl looked down. "Fasten your seat belt. You want to be safe." Mrs. Miller reached up and turned on the radio. "A little music's always nice. This air conditioning is nice, Sid."

In the canyon the boulders, brush, and ledges threw dark half-shadows. The creek was dry. The dust from the two pickups filled the bottom of the narrow canyon. Three times they passed the white skeletons of sheep.

"Coyotes," the sheriff said. "Three or four of them got into Ed Vincent's herd a couple of years ago and raised hell. He was bringing 'em off the high country for the winter. Bones don't stink, though. That's something."

The sheriff sucked his teeth. "Good cake, Maude."

The sheriff turned to look at Carl, then back at the narrow road.

"People freeze to death out in this desert in the winter. Did you know that, Carl? Mostly they get lost and die of thirst in the summer, but they can sure freeze too. Most people think the desert's always hot, but it ain't. In the summer folks have sunstrokes, of course. They even get bit by rattlesnakes once in a while, but that don't kill anybody usually. Mostly they go to sleep and smash into each other on the freeway going to Las Vegas or Disneyland. People try about every way there is to die. They're worse than sheep. We see a lot of that, don't we, Maude?"

"That's right. We surely do. People are funny."

"You'd be surprised, Carl, how many kids die out in this desert in a year. They nearly all come from big cities like Los Angeles and San Francisco. We even get some from New York. I don't know what they expect to find out here, but they sure don't know much about the desert, most of them. A bunch find a water hole and camp and smoke pot all day, and then you have to go in and tell them to wear clothes. Boys and girls both. They're nuts." The sheriff shook his head.

"They'd be a lot better off staying home with their friends and families," Mrs. Miller said. "Life's hard enough as it is."

They drove out of the narrow canyon onto a flat. On the far side, past a row of bare concrete foundations, stood an adobe cabin and sheds, with one tree for shade. On the opposite side was the mine dump, and above that the ruined tipple and the black opening of the mine shaft.

"Well, looks like we're here. You need a dog to run out and meet you, Carl. Wouldn't be so lonely then."

They parked in front of the cabin. Mrs. Miller took the plastic bottle, and Bert followed her into the cabin with the large black suitcase. When Mrs. Miller and the deputy came back out, the sheriff and Carl had pulled two sawhorses into the shade and were unloading the lumber. The toolbox sat on the ground.

"You need to fix that old generator so you'd have lights in that cabin. You'd be able to see to keep the dust cleaned out then. It's dark in there. You could have a radio and a hi-fi to enjoy. Too bad a TV won't work up this canyon." Mrs. Miller looked across at the sun on the western horizon. The south side of the canyon was deeply shadowed. "Well, we better get a move on. Building a box don't take a lot of time, if you know how. How tall would you say Richard was, Carl?"

Mrs. Miller showed them how to mark the lumber. When the bottom was cleated, she had Carl drill holes to let the water out.

"Don't want Richard swimming when we get there. Going all the way to Nephi, we'll need a foot of ice. I'll just go in now and put a bucket of water on the butane to heat and get my things ready."

When Mrs. Miller came back out, the box sat on the two sawhorses. The sheriff and the deputy were just finishing the rack to keep the boy's body off the ice. Mrs. Miller walked over and looked down into the box. The cleated lid lay against the sawhorses.

"That's a good job done." She ran her hand along the side. I've seen 'em buried in a lot worse. We used a machinery packing case once for a little boy. It was a good, strong box. Was all we had. But that was forty years ago."

She shook her head. "Well, let's go get Richard, I guess." Long dark shadows lay across the yard. Mrs. Miller looked at her watch and at the late afternoon sun. She shook her head.

The sheriff turned. "Bert, you stay here and finish that rack and listen for the radio. You sure don't get much rest in this business, Carl. We'll take your truck."

"Where's the seat belts, Carl?" Mrs. Miller said after they go in. She felt behind her on the seat and then settled back. "We'll have to dig those out before we leave."

Carl backed out the small yellow pickup and started up the grade to the shaft, the fine dust holding in the air behind them. Mrs. Miller bent forward to look up through the windshield.

"I'll bet a dozen outfits have owned this mine since the vein pitched out. I was just a little girl then. You need air conditioning, Carl."

They drove around the dump and up around the back of the tipple. The shadowed entrance to the mine shaft was a black hole in the mountain. Mrs. Miller shook her head.

"It makes you sad to think that Richard died alone in the dark. People like somebody around. It seems to make it all more worthwhile. Richard's mother will always be sad about that. Thank the good Lord that I was with my boy Billy every minute. She turned to Carl. "You had lots of relatives die, Carl?"

Carl didn't turn to look at Mrs. Miller. "No."

"I guess you're not old enough yet. Been around dead bodies much?"

Carl kept looking straight at his hand on top of the steering wheel. "No."

"Guess you haven't been to many funerals either, have you?" Mrs. Miller shook her head. "When I was a little girl I helped my mother fill our empty fruit jars with ice and pack them around the body to keep it cool for the funeral. We always washed the bottles before we put them back on the shelf. In those days some ranchers dug graves and did the burying right on the place. You sure learned what dying meant.''

They pulled up on the flat between the shaft and the tipple.

"Might as well back right up to it," the sheriff said. "We'll be loading him. There's his bike, Maude."

The red dirt bike stood parked in front of the shaft.

"Poor boy."

"We might as well load it now. He won't be using it anymore."

After they had the bike tied down, the sheriff checked the saddlebags. "Oreos, candy, five cans of pop, and a bag of those big firecrackers. We're lucky he didn't find any dynamite. There's some of it laying around these old mines."

Mrs. Miller smoothed her apron with both hands. "These old mines are nothing but death traps, nothing but death traps. Some of them have rats as big as jackrabbits and who knows what else."

She handed Carl the blanket from the pickup. The sheriff lit the Coleman lantern and led the three of them down the shaft in a circle of light. "Nice and cool in here, Carl, even if it is dark. Knew a man once who stayed in the Old Apache Mine for twenty years. Got so he could see better in the dark than he could outside, just like a bat. He must have died inside. We went back twice, but we never did find him. He got so dirty and dusty, he looked just like a rock. These old mine shafts are like those catacombs."

The sheriff's voice echoed into the darkness down the shaft. He lifted the lantern so it played more on the roof. The roof timbers all sagged. "The state ought to dynamite all these old, worked-out mines."

When they stepped on the ties between the ore-car rails, the small, brittle rocks cracked under their shoes.

"There he is, poor darling."

The sheriff lifted the lantern, the light catching the white bottoms of the boy's Keds. He lay face down between the wall and the rail. The heavy slab of rock that had killed him covered his left shoulder and arm. The blood spreading down from the collar of the light blue T-shirt was black. The sheriff raised the lantern to look at the roof and then lowered it. The boy's right hand still held the small miner's pick. The sheriff held the lantern out over the boy, spreading the light.

"Broke his neck more'n likely. Looking for gold." The sheriff shook his head. "You didn't move anything did you, Carl?"

The sheriff turned and looked at Carl.

"The sheriff asked you if you moved anything, Carl." Mrs. Miller looked at him.

"No."

"Good."

The sheriff knelt down by the boy's head and set the lantern on the ground, making the circle of light smaller..

"Damn these old gold mines anyway. About all they do is bankrupt a man or kill him, or maybe cripple him for life. Gold could go up to a thousand an ounce, and you still couldn't make them pay."

"Oh, his mother will miss him." Mrs. Miller knelt down by the sheriff, her upper body coming down into the light. She shook her head. "He's beyond our help now."

"We've sure seen our share of this kind of thing, ain't we, Maude? A kid like this ain't scared of getting killed like the rest of us. Hell, I had reports of him riding that bike of his at night on these back roads going seventy miles an hour."

With both hands the sheriff tipped the slab of rock back off the boy.

"Take his feet, Carl, and we'll turn him over." The sheriff looked up at Carl. "Just kneel down and take his feet. Give Maude the blanket."

Mrs. Miller reached out and took the blanket. She set it down and lifted the lantern, the light spreading farther into the darkness. Carl knelt down and helped lift the boy and turn him over.

"Oh, he's a beautiful boy." Mrs. Miller reached up to smooth back the boy's hair with her free hand. The eyes were closed, the mouth half open. The front of the Levi's was dark with urine.

The sheriff nodded his head toward the boy. "That happens sometimes, Carl. And sometimes worse. Maude and me have seen some messes. After a day of that desert sun, the smell can knock your hat off at half a mile. You believe in vultures then. All you can do is put 'em in a plastic bag and try to drive fast enough to stay ahead of the smell. You don't worry about getting 'em cleaned up then, I can tell you that."

Mrs. Miller put the lantern back down and took a long strip of cloth out of her apron pocket, pulled it up under the boy's jaws and around his head and tied it tight. "Morticians like you to do that. I'm glad his eyes are closed. I always feel better." Mrs. Miller patted the boy's hand.

The sheriff picked up the blanket. "Let's spread this out. We got to get going. Probably got another call by now. Always something happening. You'd think people would slow down and enjoy life a little more."

The sheriff and Carl lifted the boy onto the spread blanket and wrapped it around him.

"Now you take the shoulders and I'll take the feet, Carl. Lift." They rose together. "Good. Now take it easy."

"You be careful of your high blood pressure, Sid."

"I'm just fine."

Holding the Coleman lantern, the light moving the darkness back, Mrs. Miller led them out of the shaft. "Oh, it's nice to get back out here in the light of day," she said.

They put the boy in the back of the pickup. Mrs. Miller told Carl to ride down with the boy to be sure the dirt bike didn't break loose and tip over on him. They had to leave the tailgate flat. The sun, turned dark gold, hung just above the mountains on the west side of the flat valley. Both sides of the canyon lay in dark shadow now.

At the cabin the sheriff filled out the death certificate and the permit to transport the body. The boy lay on the table. Mrs. Miller had turned off the burner under the bucket of water. The sheriff had received a call while he was at the mine shaft. A semitruck loaded with sheep had turned over on the freeway five miles east of the junction.

"We'd like to stay and help you, Carl, but Maude's all the help you need. The box is all finished, and she'll help you wash Richard up and get him into some clean clothes. A blanket's all right if you've got a station wagon and don't have far to go. I've seen bodies hauled out on luggage racks or in trunks. It all depends on the circumstances, I guess. I saw one wrapped in tar paper once. But a good box with ice is best. You don't get so many questions when you stop for gas, and the family always appreciates the little extra things you do."

The sheriff stood up. He folded the death certificate and the permit and put them in Carl's shirt pocket. He buttoned the flap. Carl looked down at his pocket.

"Don't lose 'em. You might get arrested." The deputy laughed. "You know, Carl, you ought to get a girlfriend up here to help you keep this place dusted. You could go for long walks in the evening." The sheriff and the deputy both laughed. "Be sure to bring all of Richard's things, Maude. That's important."

"I will. Stop at the house and get another piece of that cake. And when you phone Richard's folks, would you phone Mae and tell her we'll need a nice lunch? She said to be sure and let her know if we had to go far."

"We will. That's awful good cake."

"Don't let the cats out. The coyotes could get 'em in a minute after dark."

"We'll be careful." Mrs. Miller walked out on the cabin porch to wave good-bye.

Mrs. Miller came back into the cabin and stood by the boy on the table. "That Sheriff Wilson is a good man. You wouldn't know he's got blood pressure. He's always willing to help out anybody in trouble. Lots of grief in this life." She shook her head. "Poor boy." With her hand she smoothed the boy's hair back out of his closed eyes. "It will be the sorrow of his mother's life that she ever let him come to this desert." She untied the piece of cloth around the boy's head. "There, that feels better. People ask me ahead to lay 'em out. They all want to look as nice as possible." She patted the boy's head. "Has Richard got any clean clothes, Carl? We got to get a move on. They'll be expecting us at the junction in an hour or so. It's getting darker in here. What do you use for light? Candles? Show me where the clean clothes are."

After she got the clean clothes laid out, Mrs. Miller wiped off the counter by the table. "Dust," she said, "dust." From her black suitcase on the bunk, she took an aluminum washbasin, a large sponge, a plastic hand-soap box, two heavy towels, three cloths made from heavy toweling, a white ironed sheet, a black comb, a small sewing kit, and a pair of scissors. She took out a small portable radio, turned it to a gospel-music station and set it on the counter.

"I always bring my own things. You never know what you're going to find."

Mrs. Miller leaned forward a little to look at the alarm clock on the shelf above the counter.

"Your clock's stopped." She picked it up, wound it, and then set it by her watch. She held it up to her ear. She tapped it several times on the edge of the counter and held it to her ear again. "That's all it took." She wiped the clock off with her apron and set it back on the shelf. "Time's important."

Mrs. Miller poured water from the bucket into the washbasin and set the bucket back on the unlit butane burner.

"The worst accident we ever had was an airliner crash. We had morticians from as far away as Los Angeles for that one. You can still see the hole on the way into the junction. That was the same spring the big blizzard hit and froze half the sheep on the desert. They'd all been sheared. Terrible. Nothing the ranchers could do. That was ten years ago, but you can still find thousands of sheep skeletons in some places. Nothing as dumb as a sheep."

Mrs. Miller moved down to where Carl stood at the end of the table. "You take off his shoes and socks first." She stood and watched him unlace the Keds and take them off. "Now the socks, Carl. Too bad you haven't got one of these portable radios. You could have nice music." She took off the boy's watch and set it on the counter. "Poor dear won't need that now."

When they had undressed the boy, Mrs. Miller took the folded sheet from the counter and handed one end to Carl. "This is to cover him while we wash him. Morticians do that. You have to be respectful."

Mrs. Miller pulled on the edge of the sheet to straighten it.

"Sometimes it's terrible just getting the clothes off. More than once I've had to cut off every piece. Once I had a hippie that they found frozen, his arms and legs wrapped around a cedar tree. I guess he thought the tree would keep him warm. We had to build fires all around him to thaw him out. Hippies think the desert is wonderful. They do all kinds of funny things. Some of them don't have any clothes on to begin with, which is crazy out in this desert. But I guess they don't call them hippies anymore. What do they call them, Carl? They think the desert is always warm. They wander around till they get lost. Fred was always good at finding lost people. The sheriff always took him along. Oh, I do miss my Fred." Mrs. Miller looked at Carl. "Fred got as thin as you are the last two or three months. Cancer's awful stuff."

Carl rubbed his arm with his hand.

Mrs. Miller looked at her watch and then up at Carl's clock. "We've got to get a move on. I'll wash and you do the drying. That's the quickest way when there's two of you. We'll do his back first, so let's turn him over. Be sure to get him good and dry."

Mrs. Miller wet the sponge in the warm water and soaped it. She pushed the sheet down and washed the dry blood off the boy's neck and upper back. She washed behind his ears.

"He's very clean. Sometimes I've had to use kitchen cleanser or gasoline. You just can't believe how dirty some men get working around machines or in these worthless mines. Old bachelor ranchers are just as bad. You'd think they lived in caves. It makes a big difference if a man lives with a woman, I know that. Takes a woman to keep a man clean."

Mrs. Miller pushed the sheet to the side and picked up Richard's hand. She washed the arm and hand.

"It's the feet and hands that bother you the most on a boy like this. They always do. It's not just the eyes if they're open. Be sure to get this dry down between the fingers."

She held up the hand for Carl to take.

"It's just terrible, a fine boy like this. It isn't so bad when old people like me go. We've had our lives, and we've got as many on the other side as we have here. But of course we hang on too, as long as we can, usually. Most of us still enjoy life a little anyway."

Mrs. Miller pushed the sheet up.

"Carl, I don't know what you expect to find up this canyon unless it's gold, and that's all gone years ago, as any fool knows. You need to find a good job or go to college maybe, be with your friends and family. A little wife and a nice new baby would give you something to think about. Get between the toes good."

She washed the boy's other arm, and then she stood watching Carl.

"That's right. You do a fine job. That's a good job done."

Mrs. Miller took the towel from Carl and put it in a black plastic bag she took from her suitcase.

"We're lucky you found Richard so soon. I've got a spray a mortician in Las Vegas gave me for smell, but it don't always help. That smell can come right out through the plastic and the zipper on those mortician's bags. I've seen people pour on whole bottles of shaving lotion and perfume, but it don't help. A whole ton of ice won't help either. It's the desert heat that does it so quickly. I get the spray in five-gallon cans."

Mrs. Miller picked up the clean undershorts and the T-shirt from the bunk. "Take the sheet off and put it in the bag. It's getting darker in here. We got to hurry a little bit. That music's nice this evening, isn't it?"

She put the shorts on the boy.

"There. It always makes you feel better when boys and men have their underwear on. You think they feel more comfortable. Some people don't wear underwear, of course. Hippies don't. I always carry extra in my suitcase. Families give me underwear sometimes, but some families keep everything afterward even if they don't need it."

Mrs. Miller cut the T-shirt up the back with her scissors, put it on the boy, and then they turned him over, and she stitched it up the back. She did the same with the dress shirt.

"Morticians have shirts especially made that tie at the back. You have to know what you're doing."

Mrs. Miller put the pants on the boy. "There you are, Richard. You're almost done." Looking down at him, she shook her head. "Mae helped me lay out my Billy, but I did most of it." She picked up the black comb from the counter and handed it to Carl. "You comb his hair while I put on his shoes and socks. You know how it looked better than I do."

Carl looked down at the comb.

"Go on. You know how it looked. Just hold him under the neck and lift his head a little. That's right. That looks nice. Now put the comb back on the counter and get his tie. A mother likes her boy to wear a tie. It makes him look like he's ready for church. Richard has nice clothes."

She watched Carl knot the tie. "That's right. Not many men can do that on somebody else. That looks nice." She tied the band around the boy's head to hold his mouth closed. "There."

Mrs. Miller got the gallon plastic bottle from the counter. "I make a solution to keep the skin from discoloring. It's my grandmother's recipe. I've made cloths just for this. In this heat you need heavy toweling that won't dry out every ten minutes." Mrs. Miller soaked the cloths and wrung them out. She spread one over the boy's face and wrapped each of his hands in one. "We'll have to stop every hour on the way to Nephi to keep these good and damp."

Mrs. Miller picked up the pan of dirty water and walked to the door and threw it out into the yard. Coming back in, she wiped the pan out and put it in her suitcase with her other things. She turned off her radio and put that in and had Carl take her suitcase out.

"Well, let's get Richard's things gathered up," she said when he came back. That sun's going down. They'll be expecting us. The whole canyon's dark already."

Under the boy's clean clothes in the drawer, Mrs. Miller found two girlie magazines.

"Well, we'll just leave these here. Never telling what a boy Richard's age will collect, but his poor mother doesn't need to see everything. You have to do what you can to help the living. It's best to check his wallet and his pockets too. You never can tell. Oh, I've kept more than one wife and mother from seeing what they shouldn't. Men are just men, of course, and nothing else. You can't expect perfection in this life."

Mrs. Miller had Carl pull two small cardboard boxes out from under the boy's bed while she checked the wallet, which she had taken out of the boy's Levi's earlier. One box was full of candy and cookies; the other held half a sack of firecrackers.

"We might as well leave these here. Richard's poor mother wouldn't want to see them now." She put the candy and cookies on the shelf by the clock. "You might as well enjoy them." She put the two magazines on the shelf. "Take Richard's suitcase and dirty clothes out now, Carl."

Carl carried out the suitcase and the plastic bag and came back.

"Now you can shave and put on a clean shirt, and we'll go. You can use what warm water's left there in the bucket. I'll just sit and rest for a minute."

Mrs. Miller pulled a chair up alongside the table and sat down. She rested her right arm on the table.

"I do get tired these days. Mae calls me every day. She just had her gall bladder out last month, but she's feeling better now. She's ten years younger than I am. I won't answer some day, and she'll come over and there I'll be. She knows what to do. I've told her. We've been friends for fifty years. Her husband's gone too. My will's all made out, and I've been cleaning out my closets and drawers for over a year now. I've got a list of who's supposed to get what. That's the only way. But I'm not going till the good Lord calls me home. I still like it here. You only live once."

Talking, Mrs. Miller watched Carl standing at the washstand looking into the mirror. He touched his face with both his hands.

"It'll feel good to get those off, Carl. You've got a clean shirt, haven't you? Can you see to shave? It's so dark in here. Use that warm water out of the bucket."

Mrs. Miller reached up to pat the boy on the shoulder. She shook her head.

"You don't know the things some people leave behind, sometimes whole rooms of boxes, sacks, and trunks. I've spent whole days helping to clean out just two-room shacks. People like to put things in shoe boxes and tie string around them. They hide their money in coffee cans. They do funny things. The summer before Fred died, a couple got gassed in their house trailer, and Fred found over five thousand dollars in cash in a kitchen drawer. They were wealthy people from Los Angeles. Both their poodles and their parakeet got gassed. It's awful when people die alone, and their pets stay locked up in the house with them until some neighbor or relative comes along. Cats are worse than dogs about bothering people. I guess cats forget easier. Still, cats are good companions. You ought to have a nice dog, Carl."

She looked up at him.

"I swear I can see bones. I never seen a man so thin and not dead."

Carl stood in front of the dresser pulling on a clean shirt over his T-shirt. He combed his hair.

"You look a lot better," Mrs. Miller said. She stood up and took the boy's watch from the counter. "Here, put this on till we get to Nephi. We'll need a watch we can see in the dark." She looked down at her lifted wrist. "You can't see Fred's in the dark, but it will do me what time I got left. You ought to get a nice watch, Carl."

She sat back down.

"Did you get that death certificate and that permit?" She watched him take the folded papers from his dirty shirt. "You don't want to forget them. Well, you better carry Richard out. Be careful those cloths don't fall off. I'll sure be glad to get that ice."

Carl carried the boy out and laid him in the box. Mrs. Miller showed Carl how to tack the lid on. He slid the box off of the sawhorses and onto the pickup. Because he had to leave the tailgate flat, Mrs. Miller told him he'd better tie the box down.

"There, that's a good job done."

They got in the pickup. Mrs. Miller fished behind her for her seat belt, then sat forward on the seat.

"Where are they, Carl? You need 'em on a long trip." She reached down between the seat and the back and pulled out her belt. "There. Now you get yours." She sat back in the seat, pulled the belt tight, and snapped it.

The red desert sun was setting behind the distant edge of the black mountains as they pulled away from the cabin. All the shadows were gone. The canyon was dark, the row of cement foundations pale white. Mrs. Miller brought her right wrist up close to her face to look at her watch. They passed the little cemetery.

"Lonely place to be buried, Carl. That cemetery was down toward the end. They put it too close to the creek. After the cloudburst my father and some of the other men spent a whole day digging new graves to bury the bones they gathered downstream. You'll have to go slow on this road. We don't want Richard bumping his head. Keeps the dust down a little too."

Mrs. Miller turned to look out the back window.

"I always feel better when we've got the ice. You think they feel better too. Air conditioning in a pickup makes life a lot more enjoyable out on this desert."

Mrs. Miller rested her left hand on the plastic bottle on the seat between them. When she took her hand off, the bottle fell against Carl. He looked down at it. They crossed the dry creekbed and drove off the flat and down into the dark canyon, the dust rising behind them. Carl turned on the headlights.

"That's better."

Mrs. Miller reached up and turned on the radio. She turned up the volume and then turned the dial. "Your radio doesn't work, Carl." She hit the radio several times hard with her fist. The dial light came on, and she found a music station. She adjusted the volume. "There. You just had a loose connection."

Carl turned to look at her.

On a curve the headlights hit two skeletons. "Sheep." Mrs. Miller shook her head.

The dogs ran down the lane to meet them when they got to Mrs. Miller's place. The truck stopped in the circle of light under the lamppost. Mrs. Miller told Carl to bring in her things, except for the hammer. While Mrs. Miller got ready, she had Carl water her geraniums. She fed and watered the cats, dogs, chickens, and parakeets.

"I've already fed the fish," she said. "Mae will have a nice lunch for us, but I'd better eat a banana. I don't want my diabetes acting up. Do you want something, Carl? I've got my insulin and pills."

"No."

"Well, you might later."

Mrs. Miller cut a big wedge of the chocolate cake and put it in a plastic container with a lid. She left the lamp and the swamp cooler on. the three dogs ran ahead of them until Mrs. Miller called their names and told them to go back.

The road out across the sagebrush valley was smoother than the canyon road, and Mrs. Miller told Carl to drive faster. Sometimes when they came to the tops of low hills, far ahead was a ranch house with a light hanging from the top of a twenty-foot-high lamppost casting a circle of light out into the road. At each ranch house Mrs. Miller had Carl blink his headlights, and then she watched in the rearview mirror until a pickup pulled out. Every time Mrs. Miller took her hand off the plastic bottle, it fell against Carl. She reached up to adjust the radio.

"We don't ever have time for a funeral when something sudden like this happens, but folks like to pay their respects. It's about all they can do, I guess."

They passed the fifth ranch house, Carl blinking the lights as they approached the lamppost.

"Out there that's where that airliner crashed." Mrs. Miller pointed out into the darkness. "There were bodies and parts of that plane scattered for two miles. We had twenty men out there with shotguns just to keep the vultures and ravens away. Everybody helps at a time like that. We used barns for morgues. We had a dump truck bringing ice for two days as fast as he could go. It was hot. Right in the middle of summer. July."

The small yellow pickup led a procession of six vehicles, about two hundred yards between them because of the dust. Ahead, the traffic on the freeway was steady; the glow of light on the other side was the junction. They drove through the underpass and made the turn. The attendant standing at the Chevron-station door waved. Mrs. Miller waved.

"You know Hal, don't you? He's run that station for twenty years. Not much business, though, since the freeway came through. Just enough to live on."

They left the circle of light in front of the station and entered the light spreading out from the store. A dozen cars and pickups stood parked in front of the store. People stood silhouetted on the long porch, the two big, square store windows lit behind them, a large, lit Coca-Cola clock above the door. Two large blocks of ice lay at the top of the steps, dripping water.

"They left a space for you, Carl, there by the steps. Just back in."

As Carl turned to back in, the five pickups that had been following him drove around and parked at the far end of the porch at the edge of the light.

"That's good."

Six people standing on the porch held up their hands for him to stop. Mrs. Miller got out.

"Come on, Carl."

Mrs. Miller waited for Carl to walk around to her side of the pickup. He followed her up the steps. People said hello quietly.

"Mel, you know Carl here?"

"Why sure. He's been in the store."

Mel shook his hand. Other people held out their hands. Two of the men reached up to pat him on the back.

"It's a terrible thing for a boy that young to get killed." Mel shook his head. "Why he was just in the store yesterday playing the pinball machines and enjoying himself. He must have had three Cokes and a couple of ice-cream cones. This desert is no place for anybody with any sense. I keep telling my wife that. Raising a family's hard enough as it is."

Other people nodded.

"Well, we better get the ice in that box, Mel. This weather's hot even after the sun goes down."

Mel and three other men helped Carl slide the box out. Mel's wife swept off the dust before Carl loosened the nails on the lid. Mrs. Miller leaned over the box to take off the soaked pads and the headband before Mel and Carl lifted Richard out. Mel's wife and another woman had spread a blanket on the porch.

"That's what happens when you play in old gold mines," she said. "You kids remember it. He's broke his mother's heart, you can depend on that."

Mrs. Miller knelt down and brushed the boy's hair back with her hand.

"Such a nice looking boy, Maude."

"Any mother would enjoy having a fine boy like that."

"Yes, she would."

Mel cut one of the blocks of ice in two with an ice pick and lifted the two halves into the box. He gave Carl an ice pick and showed him how to chip the ice.

"You did a good job on this box, Carl. People always forget to allow for the water, don't they, Maude?"

"Yes, they do." Mrs. Miller looked toward the gas station. "Well, looks like Hal's got at least one customer tonight." Carl and Mel both looked up.

A man and woman walked across the yard from the pumps, where Hal was cleaning the windshield on a big red Lincoln Continental. The woman, a blonde who wore orange shorts and a white halter, was wobbly on her high heels in the gravel. The tall bald man wore a bright yellow, flowered shirt. They entered the light at the end of the porch and climbed the steps there. The woman flicked her half-smoked cigarette away and folded her arms across her chest. The man put his arm around her waist. A woman in a blue housedress turned and spoke to her. They both shook their heads, and then the blonde woman said something to the man.

"Two hundred pounds ought to get you to Nephi okay, Maude. They ought to refrigerate those hearses and put four-wheel drive on 'em for this country. There'd be plenty of business."

Mel helped Carl lift Richard back into the box. Mrs. Miller soaked the cloths and wrung them out.

"Maude does that for color," Mae said to the crowd.

"Just drive those nails a little more than halfway, Carl," Mrs. Miller said. "Richard's family will want to see him as soon as we get to Nephi."

"We'd invite you in for supper, Maude, but we know you got to get going." Mel turned to his wife. "Nancy's got a nice sack of apples for you. It's something you can eat, Maude." Mel's wife held out a plastic sack of red apples.

"Thank you, Mel. Mae's fixed us a nice lunch."

"I already put it on the seat. Always glad to help. I'll go by your place tomorrow and check on things and do the feeding."

"That ice is on the house, Maude. We can do that much."

"I'll tell the family. They'll appreciate all your help. We'll call you as soon as we get there, Mel. Thanks."

"We'll expect to see you both for church Sunday maybe."

Carl turned to look at Mel.

The men on the porch reached out to shake Carl's hand and pat him on the shoulder. People waved to them as they drove over to the gas pumps, and Mrs. Miller waved back. Hal was handing the man in the red Lincoln Continental his change as they drove up. Hal stepped back and the Lincoln drove out to the road leading to the on-ramp. Hal leaned down to put his ear in Mrs. Miller's window. "Don't get out, Carl. I'll pump her for you."

While the tank filled, Hal cleaned the windshield with blue paper towels and a spray bottle. He leaned back to talk to Mrs. Miller. "That blonde in the Continental sure was broken up, Maude."

"I could see she had a kind face. Probably lost a boy of her own or maybe a little brother."

"She was bawling and trying to light a cigarette when they pulled out of here. That guy was patting her on the shoulder and saying something to her."

"Poor dear."

Hal went around to do the other side of the windshield. "Two years ago, Carl, I had a woman drive in here for gas with her husband sitting straight up in his seat. He'd had a heart attack and died. She was taking him home that way. I asked if she wanted a sheet or something to cover him with, but she said it would look funny. She had the shoulder strap on him tight, so of course he sat up straight. She only had fifty miles to go. They were out for a Sunday drive."

"It can happen anytime, anytime at all, Hal. We all know that." She reached over to pat Carl on the knee.

Hal topped off the tank and came back around to Mrs. Miller's side. "No charge, Carl. These little Jap trucks don't take much gas. See you when you get back. Your tires look okay. Keep him awake, Maude. That ice is already melting a stream. It's real hot tonight."

"Thank you, Hal."

Mrs. Miller turned to wave to Hal as they pulled out, leaving the pool of light. They stopped at the stop sign. The chocolate cake in the Tupperware carton, the sack of apples, Mae's lunch, and the plastic gallon bottle lay on the seat between them. Carl drove up onto the freeway. His hands were at the top of the steering wheel.

"Hal's nice. He had his stomach out for cancer a little over a year ago, but he still keeps that station going. He's got a wife and three kids to support."

Ahead red and yellow lights flashed.

"Better slow down. It's that truck accident Sid got the call on."

Black skid marks led off the road where the semitruck lay on its back in a gully. Two wreckers with cables worked to pull the truck upright. The dead sheep had been gathered into piles.

"Poor dumb things."

The plastic gallon bottle tipped against Carl. He reached down and set it upright. They picked up speed. A car came up behind them in the middle lane and passed. The woman sitting by the driver looked across at them. She turned to watch them, her face fading into the darkness as the car pulled ahead.

Mrs. Miller turned twice to look out the rear window.

"He's fine. Nice music, Carl." She turned up the sound a little.

A car came up behind them in their lane. After a few minutes it pulled up parallel. The car's windshield wipers were on. The woman passenger looked across at them. She turned to talk to the driver and then looked at them again. She turned to look at the box in the back of the pickup. Mrs. Miller leaned forward and waved. The woman waved. She spoke to the driver again and then turned back. She stayed turned, watching them until the car vanished into the darkness.

"People are curious about the water coming out of the box. They don't expect to have to turn on their windshield wipers in the middle of a desert. When the wind's just right it blows the water right over the cab onto your windshield. Fred would have to keep his wipers going the whole trip. Can't put your arm on the windowsill, or it'll get all wet. Sometimes you have to close the window."

Carl pulled his arm in from the window.

Mrs. Miller reached up and turned his wrist so she could see the watch. "We ought to be there on time. I don't like to get there at night in the dark, but it can't be helped this once, I suppose. You still got those papers, haven't you?" Mrs. Miller turned and patted his shirt pocket. She buttoned down the flap. "Good."

Mrs. Miller reached over and got the Tupperware and put it on her lap.

"How about your piece of chocolate cake? You never did have your piece of cake." She took off the lid. "Still smells nice and fresh." The steep desert mountains rose on either side of the freeway, cutting out the moon. "Oh, it's dark out there, nothing but darkness."

A fine mist covered the windshield. Mrs. Miller reached over and turned on the windshield wiper.

"Better have some cake, Carl." She held up the container.

He turned to look at Mrs. Miller and then looked out the windshield again. And then, without looking at Mrs. Miller, he lowered his hand from the steering wheel and took the piece of cake from the container. He took a little bite at first, and then big bites, swallowing the cake without really chewing.

Mrs. Miller reached over and patted his knee. "That's right. Enjoy it. That's what it's for. Enjoy it."

The Rooster

The jangling alarm clock woke him. He pulled his arm from under the heavy quilts and stopped it. His wife's arm, white in the moonlight coming through the windows where the blinds hung in tatters, lay across his chest. He stared at it. He could feel her heat beside him. Sleeping with her was like sleeping with a stove. He pushed her arm away. Even outside the covers in the cold, her arm felt warm, damp.

He sat up, then saw her turn over. She pushed the quilts down from her face and looked up at him, her wide, white face framed in the black twisted hair. Careful to keep his feet suspended a few inches over the icy linoleum when he pushed them out, he reached for his heavy socks on the chair. He dropped one in the shadowed darkness between the bed and the chair, cursed, and pulled the light string over his head.

"What you up for?" she asked.

"Going pheasant hunting."

She grunted. "Leave a nice warm bed to go tromp in the weeds all day; you must be crazy as hell." White in his long underwear, he balanced on one foot beside the bed and fished for the other sock. "Did you have to turn on the light?"

He didn't answer. What was the use? The only time she was happy was when she was sitting in front of the TV with a cold six-pack watching one of her love movies.

"You might show some consideration," she said. She jerked the quilts back over her head. He didn't know how she could breathe under all that bedding. She was like a fish, a damned whale.

Dressed except for his boots, he turned off the light, pulled the bolt on the door, and padded down the dark hall past the girls' room to the kitchen. When he flipped on the light, her big grey tabby cat jumped from the table, where it had been feeding among the supper dishes. He kicked but missed, and it ran down the hall to the bedroom and safety. Her and her damned cats. He couldn't have a hunting dog because of the cats. Fat chance a dog would have against that pack of tigers. Someday he was going to drop about half a pound of poisoned liver in the backyard.

The fire was out. He rubbed his hands against the cold, turned on both sides of the hot plate and put on last-night's coffee to heat. Pushing the empty beer cartons aside, he got eggs and bacon from the refrigerator. It wouldn't hurt her to get up once and fix his breakfast and make him a sandwich, show a little of that consideration she was always yapping about. But not her. She liked the bed too much.

After he ate he went out on the back porch to his cabinet for his hunting things. He unlocked the cabinet, took out his double-barrel, shells, hunting coat and hat, and boots. At the far end of the porch, his boy slept. Four girls and one boy—that was something else she had done to him; it should have been just the other way around. He laced his boots. If the oldest had been a boy, he would be old enough to go hunting now. He went back into the kitchen.

Fifteen minutes after pulling out of his yard, he was parked in the Willow Creek bottoms south of town waiting for shooting light. He smoked, watching the vapors rise along the creek and thinking about what it had been like on the creek when he was a kid. Those had been the good years—fishing, potting birds and maybe a rabbit once in a while with their slingshots, stealing corn and chickens to cook, swimming bare-assed naked all day at the hole, wild as Indians, happy. The fences, clumps of willows, and haystacks slowly took shape in the growing light.

He hadn't hunted the bottoms since he was a kid, since before he went in the navy. The best hunting was fifty miles south around the big grainfields, but today was something special. He was after a giant rooster he had seen from the road two weeks before when he had come down to buy winter potatoes. Three times as big as any of the dozen hens it was feeding with, it had stood there in the cut grainfield, its bronze breast gold in the fading sun, its twenty-inch-long tail sticking almost straight up, the only rooster in the field. He wanted that bird, wanted to jump it out of the weeds, shoot it, knock it out of the air, stop the shrill cackle. He wanted to hold it, run his fingers through the bright feathers, stroke the long tail. And he would too. Those hens were going to be mighty lonely. He smiled.

He had shooting light. He ground out his cigarette against the window and got out. He loaded his gun. Hunting alone and without a dog, he would have to stick to small cover, stuff he would work himself. Still, he had a good chance because the birds would be out feeding. Someday he would have a dog whether she squawked or not. He deserved a dog. He walked through the frosty grass, his index finger ready on the front trigger's cool metal.

He hunted the small, irrigated corn and grainfields hard for the first hour, but saw nothing of the big rooster, jumping only two hens. Soon the birds would be off the feed and into heavy cover to stay until late afternoon. The sun was up. It was going to be a warm day. He hunted for another hour, trying hard to locate that flock of hens. The rooster would be with the hens. But he saw nothing, only two or three cottontails. Finally he crossed the creek to hunt the edge of a wheatfield he'd seen from the north side. A mile or so farther down, he could see the big cottonwood tree that marked their old swimming hole. He gazed at the tree. Those had been the best years; nobody sitting on his back then.

Except for an occasional wind-drifted tumbleweed, the field was empty, the stubble like yellow grass in the brilliant sunlight. No birds fed along the edges as he had expected. He hunted a patch of grass at the end of the field and started jumping hens, one right after the other. His heart pounded. Zigzagging through the grass, gun at the ready, he was sure he had the big rooster now. He pushed off the safety. But the rooster didn't jump, just the brown hens rocketing up and whirring away to heavy cover. He worked the grass again, sure the rooster was still there. No luck. "Hell," he said to himself softly. Not having a bird down by this time, even if it wasn't the big rooster, was bad. He couldn't figure out how he had missed him. Taking off his hat he ran his fingers through his itchy, sweat-sticky hair. It was hot.

For the next two hours he bucked the heavy cover, working the sloughs along the creek and the patches of heavy weeds, some of the stuff shoulder high and like a brick wall, knowing all the while it was next to hopeless. He swore every time he thought about not having a dog; it would be so easy with a dog. He did get up one bird, a small this-year's rooster, but blew it all to hell because he shot too soon. He didn't even bother to pick it up.

At noon he quit. He took off the heavy coat and sat in the shade of a willow clump near the creek, his shirt damp with sweat. He ate his sandwich, washing down the throat-sticking bread with the warm thermos coffee. She would expect him home about one o'clock to take her downtown to get the Saturday groceries, and already she was sniffing around for Christmas presents. Not November yet, and she was thinking about Christmas.

It was bad going home without a couple of birds. She would give him the raspberry. She liked pheasant. He thought about it for a while, and finally decided he wasn't going home. He wasn't going back without birds whether she got to town or not. He would wait for the late-afternoon shooting. He ate his apple, then lay back on his folded coat. It would do her good to walk. He could just see her going up and down the store aisles, looking at things, lifting this, touching that, the kids trailing behind her. She was worse than any kid.

When he woke, the sun was still high, and he knew he hadn't slept more than an hour. He looked through his coat to see if there might be a piece of candy or something left over from a previous hunt. There wasn't. He lit a cigarette. He had about two hours to wait. He could wait. Then down the creek he saw the big cottonwood by the old hole, and he knew what he would do. He would go down and see what it looked like. He hadn't been back in years. It would be fun, something to do. The town kids didn't come down here anymore; they all used the city pool.

He walked slowly at first, but then faster, like when they were kids and started to run the last couple of hundred yards, hollering insults about the last one to pull off his clothes and jump in. Then he pushed through the last red willows and dropped down into the little basin surrounding the hole.

Just as he thought; it hadn't changed. It was like he was a kid again. He took off his coat, set his gun down on it, and walked down to the long, wide pool. The same gnarled willow tree still hung out from the bank. They had dived from there. Damn, they'd had fun swimming, diving, playing tag, yelling—their naked, wet bodies flashing in the sun. It seemed strange to him that a tree would not change, but just be there like it always was, and he had to get older, and things be different.

The pile of rocks was still there. Every spring they dug out the hole a little, dumping the rocks on the bank in piles. Dead grass and weeds tangled around the rocks. He walked over and picked one up, hefted it, wondered if he might have dropped it there fifteen years before. Then he picked up another, and another, but he knew he couldn't tell, so he stopped. The big cottonwood was across the creek. He knew his initials were carved in it, but he didn't want to see now.

He went back to his coat, sat down, and began idly throwing pebbles into the water, watching the ripples until they faded, and then throwing again. He was hungry. She should have packed him a good lunch, but no, not her. He decided he would shoot a cottontail and cook it. It would be like when he was a kid.

Fifteen minutes later he was back with a rabbit. All the wood around the hole was too soft for hot coals, so he walked down the creek to a stand of scrub oak he remembered. The white skeleton of a sheep near the oak reminded him of something, and he laughed. They had hidden in the oak once to watch a farmer turn the rams in to a flock of ewes. At first they had just watched, but then they had begun to shoot the ewes with their slingshots whenever a ram got interested.

That had been fun. There the ram was, all ready, and then the ewe went running off, leaving the ram just standing around with the dumbest look on his face. Finally, the farmer saw them and chased them away. He hadn't seen them shooting; just said it was nothing for young boys to be watching. They laughed about that all the way home.

He tied the rabbit on the spit with a piece of fence wire and suspended it over the hot coals on two forked sticks. He turned it occasionally, but he wasn't watching the rabbit. He was watching the movement of the water in the hole, the slow, circular motion before it funneled out again at the bottom. The sun and the fire warmed him. He tried to bring it all back, see them there as kids, find the feeling he'd had then. He seemed almost to be reaching out for it.

Suddenly he wanted to go swimming again, like when he was a kid. It would be cold, but he had the sun and the fire, and there wasn't any wind. He began to take off his clothes. When he had his pants off, he hesitated and stood to full height in his long, white underwear to make sure nobody was around. Then he pulled off his underwear.

Naked, he stood looking down at himself. He was white, and his belly was soft. He had been brown then, hard muscled, his belly flat without sucking it in, like a statue. Marrying too early ruined a man. Thirty-five was plenty early enough. If it hadn't been for her old man putting up such a squeal, he wouldn't have married so young. It'd been a false alarm anyway. He shouldn't have scared so easy. If he laid off the beer for a while, he could get back into shape.

He stepped into the water up to his ankles, then stopped. It was colder than he'd thought. Sand pushed up between his toes and drifted away in the current. He walked in deeper, the clear water distorting his white legs and feet. The water numbed him. When it reached his thighs he stopped again, sucking in his breath. Just for a second he was tempted to dive in all at once, like they used to in the spring, daring each other—but he didn't. He might catch pneumonia. It would be better to come back in the summer, bring his boy. A kid shouldn't miss this. He backed out of the water, careful not to splash.

He didn't dress. It was better to crouch before the fire, feeling the heat against his skin, to bake a little and dry. They always did that. He built up the fire. The rabbit was done. He took it off the spit and began to eat, breaking the parts off with his fingers, tasting the burned outside flesh, pulling the white pieces from the bones. The grease and juice smeared his hands, and small drops fell on his paunchy stomach, catching in the body hair. Naked, crouched there, he ate the whole rabbit, throwing the white bones into the fire, where they smoked and turned brown.

After he finished, he dressed and then lay back on his coat in the grass to sleep, his hat over his eyes, his belly full and warm. He still had an hour.

When he woke up, the sun was already dropping toward the west mountains. Stiff but rested, he stood erect. The tall clumps of willows cast long shadows across the uneven ground and the squat blue sagebrush. It was quiet. The fire smoldered, the rabbit bones black now.

After he got back to the planted fields, he started hunting, working the cover along the edges of the fields, hoping to pick up a bird. And slowly he made his way back to the grainfield where he had jumped the hens that morning. The big rooster had to be around somewhere close, with that many hens in one spot. As he neared the field, the sun was an orange ball resting on the rim of the west mountains.

The big rooster and about a dozen hens were feeding in the stubble near a patch of grass. The rooster was even bigger than he had remembered, the breast black from that distance, the tail stiff in the air. Seeing him, the birds crouched and ran into the high grass. He made a circle, coming in on the far side so as to block the rooster if it ran once it was shielded by the high grass. His breath coming quick from the run and the excitement, he began to work the grass, sure that he had the big rooster trapped now. But he jumped only hens. Puzzled, he worked the grass again. Still no rooster. He stood for a moment at the edge of the grass, his gun still raised to the ready. The rooster had to be in there. He hunted the grass again, but still no bird.

Standing there, he swore to himself quietly. The rooster must have slipped through the grass and out the other side before he got around to cut him off. It was the only answer. Just too fast. He swore again, then, disappointed, crooking his gun in his arm, he walked out across the grainfield toward the car. He still had a half hour of shooting light left. Maybe he could still get one. It would be bad going home without at least one bird. She was going to be mad as hell anyway.

He jumped the big rooster from under one of the grey tumbleweeds he passed in midfield. It was pure luck, the bird bursting out almost at his feet, waiting till the last minute, then coming out, cackling shrill, straight up. Startled, he snapped his gun to his shoulder, but shot too soon and missed. Gaining speed, sweeping to the left, the giant rooster climbed. He caught it over the barrels again and pulled down. Careful. Follow through. Now. Dark feathers burst free, the head dropped, wings collapsed in tangles, and the big bird fell, crashing into the wheat stubble.

"Got ya!"

His heart pounding in his chest, he ran toward the bird. Setting his gun down, he lifted the rooster from the stubble. "Four pounds easy," he said. "Beautiful." He smoothed the feathers, the beautiful feathers, the green-blue head, the banded throat, the gold breast feathers and the long, speckled tail. He stroked the tail. He held the rooster out from him to get a better look, the last rays of the sun coloring the feathers. Smart, letting the hens decoy. Well, that was the last thing they would ever do for the big bird. Grinning, careful not to break the stiff tail, he placed the rooster gently in his large rear game pocket. It was dusk. The light blue sky had darkened, and by the time he was within sight of the car, the shadows had all faded to match the greyness. A magpie screeched from a tree. A herd of white-faced cattle grazed in the last field he had to cut through. The cows watched him. He crossed the fence and walked toward the car. A big range bull, black now in the fading light, walked to the fence to look at him closer. He hadn't seen it earlier. They could be dangerous. Once, when he was a kid, he'd crept up through the bushes on a bull like that and shot it in the bag with his BB gun. What a circus that had been. He got to the car.

Twenty minutes later he was in town driving through the Saturday-evening traffic. He was thirsty and decided to stop at the Palace, a little joint near his place, for a beer. He patted his stomach. Just one beer wasn't going to hurt him any, but all he was going to have was one. Staying away a little longer wasn't going to make any difference in how she felt. He parked. After he got out he lifted the rooster from the seat where he had laid it and put it back in his coat. Charlie would be surprised.

He pushed open the door. Charlie was at the far end of the bar drying a glass and watching two kids play pool at one of the four tables down past the booths. It was still early for there to be much of a crowd. He sat down on one of the upholstered tree stumps and faced his own distorted image in the dusty, blistered mirror across the bar. In the mirror he was surrounded by the stuffed heads of big-antlered bucks hanging on the wall behind him. Every fall Charlie gave a prize for the biggest buck. He had won six years ago. His buck was there, third from the left on the top row.

Charlie came toward him. "Well, looks like you been out. Do anything?"

He didn't answer but reached in the back of his coat, brought out the big rooster and laid it on the bar. He smoothed the feathers and arranged the head and tail.

"Say, that's really nice," Charlie said. "Big."

"Biggest one I ever shot."

The two kids came out from the back to see the bird. He ordered a beer. One of the kids stroked the back and long tail. "He's beautiful," he said.

"Your little woman was in this afternoon," Charlie said.

He took a long suck of beer from the already half-empty glass. "What did she want?"

"Bought a couple of six-packs."

He shook his head. Come hell or high water, she had to have her beer.

"Those five kids of yours are growing up."

"Hell, did she drag them in here?" He watched the white bubbles form and disappear in his glass.

"No. They stood out front. They look healthy. Must cost you plenty for groceries."

He didn't answer. Two more customers came in and sat down beside him. He told them how he had hunted the big rooster all day, finally trapping it in the grainfield. They nodded.

The place was filling up. He didn't want to leave. Nearly everyone who came in stopped to look at the rooster. Some stroked it. One woman wanted to buy the tail feathers. "I'll give you five dollars," she said. "I make hats. Don't I make hats, Harold?" She nudged a little man next to her. He nodded.

Five dollars. He looked at her. She was big. Her lipstick was painted out over the lines of her thin lips like two hearts stuck butt ends together. Her silky dress fit tight.

"How about it?" She fingered the tail feathers.

"Don't do it, buddy," a fellow on the next stool said. He had been playing a green punchboard.

"Who said you can't have your cake and eat it too?" she said, laughing. She put down her purse so she could use both hands. "Pay the man, Harold."

"I don't want to sell," he said.

She looked at him, the heart-lips tight in surprise. "You must be crazy. You can't eat the feathers, can you?"

"I don't want to sell."

She pulled her hands away. "Come on, Harold," she said. "This guy doesn't know a good thing when it stares him in the face." He watched her walk away.

"Bitch," the fellow playing the punchboard said.

Talk, the clink of glasses, and the click, click of billiard balls surrounded him. The air was a blue haze now. He took his third beer and walked back to the pool tables, leaving the rooster lying on the bar. He played pool and won. He pushed a good stick when he was feeling just right. He heard people talking about the rooster. After ordering beers for the table twice, he still came out better than three dollars ahead. When he got back to the bar, it was past nine. Nobody had taken his seat by the bird. He felt good.

The crowd was beginning to thin out some, most going to the dance at the Pavilion or to the second show. They would be back before Charlie closed to pick up their cold six-packs.

"I'll have one last one, Charlie," he said. Charlie slid the beer across to him. As he took his first swallow somebody sat down on an empty stool two away from him. He turned. It was Paul Wicket. They'd gone to school together. Paul had got shot up in the war and had a nice pension. He was single.

"A dozen of that German beer," Paul told Charlie. Then Paul saw him. "Well," he said, "I haven't seen you in quite a while." He leaned closer. "It looks like you got one."

"Ya."

Paul paid with a twenty when Charlie handed him the sack, and then stuffed the change into his pocket. "See you around," Paul said. "That's a nice bird."

Through the front window he saw Paul climb into a new red Chevy. He handed the sack to a woman sitting next to him, then leaned over and kissed her. When he pulled back to turn on the key, Paul saw him watching and waved. He turned on his lights and backed out.

"There goes the biggest skirt chaser in town," Charlie said; he had been watching Paul too. "How lucky can one guy be—money, women, and plenty to drink?"

He watched the red taillight vanish up the road. "Let me have another one, Charlie," he said. Paul had gone swimming with him sometimes. He would have liked to talk to him about that, told him that he had been back, and that the old hole on Willow Creek was the same still. You shouldn't let such things die. Paul had a good-looking woman.

He sat sipping beer. A breasty redhead in a white bathing suit looked up at him from the green punchboard on the bar. She was on a box of chocolates. It said: "Take me home—I'm sweet." He put down his beer and picked up the board. He studied it for a minute, then pulled the frayed match out of the empty hole and started to jab through the silver paper covering the unpunched holes. After ten punches he began to open the little, pressed pieces of paper. The number had to end in five. He had one winner. "It looks like I got one," he said, pushing the piece of paper across the bar to Charlie.

"That's a good board," Charlie said. "Lots of people win." Charlie checked the punch, then got one of the boxes of chocolates with the girl on the lid down from the shelf in front of the mirror. Charlie wiped the dust off the cellophane with his apron.

He sipped his beer and studied the girl on the box. Besides himself there were only a half dozen people in the place. It was quiet. He didn't like it so quiet. Then a big blonde and her boyfriend walked in. He looked up, following her in the mirror. She had on a tight green dress that glinted green light. When they sat down at the bar, she was on his side and showed two inches of white thigh getting on her stool, the tight dress swelling around her hips as she adjusted herself. They ordered beers. The straps of her dress pulled tight into her white shoulders. She was big. She turned and looked up at the bucks on the wall.

He watched her out of the corner of his eye and in the mirror. He saw her cover her boyfriend's hand when he let it slide from her shoulder down to her hip. After one beer they left, his arm so tight around her waist they rubbed together as they walked. She said something about the pretty bird as they passed.

The red-headed girl smiled up at him from the top of the box. Slowly he traced her outline with his finger, the cellophane was silky. He swallowed hard, and his hands began to sweat a little. He could feel his blood beginning to pound, hear it. He sat there staring at the figure on the box, then in one quick movement, he picked up the box of chocolates and put it in the big side pocket of his hunting coat. When he picked up the rooster, a drop of blood glistened on the bar where the head had been.

"See ya, Charlie," he said. "Got to get home."

Charlie raised a wet hand from the sink. "Goin'? Well, take 'er easy."

"See ya." He thought he smelled heavy perfume when he got close to the door. The blonde. He hurried to his car.

Driving along he could feel the box of chocolates in his side pocket. Lowering his right hand from the steering wheel, he touched the rooster that lay on the seat beside him. He stroked its feathers. It was lucky winning the chocolates; they would help. If she'd drunk three or four beers out of the six-pack, though, she would probably be in a pretty good mood. She could be as mad as hell and change just like that after a few beers. It had been that way the first time. He laughed and pushed on the gas.

Only the kitchen light was burning when he pulled into the moon-bright yard. Usually the TV lamp in the front room would be on, especially on Saturday night. She always watched the ten o'clock movie on Saturday night. But even if she was in bed, she could still be awake.

He hurried up the back steps but was careful not to slam the back screen door. He didn't want to wake the boy. She had been after him for two months to take the screens down. He would do that. He locked all his hunting things away in his closet. He would clean his gun tomorrow.

He had his story all ready in case she was up. But she wasn't. There was a note. He set the rooster and the candy on top of the clean table and picked up the note. It said: "Dear Honey, Pie in the warming oven. Plenty of hot water for a bath." It was signed "Honey."

She didn't very often leave him a note. He was surprised. He could see the bedroom door at the end of the lighted hall. It was ajar. He wanted to go right down, but he knew he hadn't better. If he didn't take the bath and eat some of the pie, she might get mad. She could hear whether he took the bath or not. She liked him to have a bath. He didn't want her mad.

As he turned to walk into the bathroom, he noticed the trash box. Five empty, gold-topped beer cans glinted there in the light. He smiled and hurried into the bathroom. He set the plug, turned on the water full force, and began to pull off his clothes. On top of the toilet was a clean set of long underwear. She'd even thought of that.

When the tub was full enough, he turned off the water and put one foot in. It was too hot. He added some cold water. He stepped in; then, grabbing the left side of the tub with one hand and cupping himself with the other, he lowered slowly, carefully into the water. He shivered when he thought of the numbing water in the swimming hole that afternoon. He must have been crazy.

Usually he liked to soak, but not tonight. He washed hurriedly and got out. He dried himself, then pulled on the long white underwear. It fit tight, just as it always did when he first put it on, showing the round outline of his paunch. He sucked in. If he was careful, he could make that muscle in six months. He knew about some exercises. He couldn't find his old blue bathrobe behind the door, only his sheepskin-lined slippers. He put them on. He thought about putting his pants back on, but decided not to. He wouldn't be in the kitchen that long.

When he opened the warming oven, he saw it was one of those supermarket pies. She didn't bake very good pies. He cut a wedge but broke it in pieces in his hurry to get it on the plate. After two bites he decided he wasn't hungry and carried what was left over to the trash box, where he buried it underneath the beer cans and a milk carton.

He was ready now. He picked up the chocolates. The rooster could stay on the table till morning. He hadn't seen any of the cats around. He had been thinking about the cats. He figured if he bought a pup it would grow up gradual and get used to the cats. He had heard of cats and dogs being friends. He would ask her about it tonight maybe.

He snapped off the kitchen light and walked down the hall, his hand already sweat slick on the cellophane-covered box, his blood pounding. He swallowed hard. He passed by the girls' open door without looking in, pausing only to turn off the hall light. He didn't see her big, grey tabby cat slip out of the door he was about to enter and slink tigerlike down the hall toward the kitchen.

He pushed the door back quietly, stepped silently in. He closed it again and pushed the bolt, fingered it to make sure. He stood waiting for his eyes to get used to the pale light of the moonlit room. He didn't want to turn the light on. She lay on the far side of the bed, her face hidden by a shadow. He couldn't tell whether she was awake or not. He stepped closer. He saw his reflection in the mirror. He didn't have a head, only a white body.

"Honey," she said, whispery.

He paused. His throat tightened again.

"I been waiting," she said. She pushed back the covers, exposing a heavy white arm cut off at the shoulder by a pink nightgown. "I been waiting."

Shifting the sweaty box of chocolates to his left hand, he reached out to touch her. He had to lean over the edge of the bed. He felt her warm, damp arm.

"Ah, honey," he said, "ah, honey."

Mr. Wahlquist in Yellowstone

Barney, the Lake district ranger, organized the search for Mr. Wahlquist to begin at first light Labor Day morning. Mr. Wahlquist had left the Fishing Bridge Trailer Court on Sunday afternoon in his red Ford pickup for Hayden Valley to look for the Central Plateau buffalo herd, which had been reported down near the main road. He hadn't come back. Hayden Valley was seven miles long and three miles wide. The main park road followed the Yellowstone River through the grassy flats and the sagebrush-covered hills. Beyond the hills rose the mountains.

I was a seasonal ranger working at Lake for the summer. In the fall I would start law school at the University of Nebraska, and this was my summer off. I should have gotten a law-office clerkship in Omaha. But I'd been to Yellowstone three or four times with my family as a kid, and I liked it. I wanted to spend one summer as a ranger.

I'd met the Wahlquists in early June on a campground check. They were from Omaha too, and nice people. I visited them in their trailer a lot. Mrs. Wahlquist liked to feed me. All through August Mrs. Wahlquist had been telling me she didn't think they would ever spend another summer in Yellowstone.

"Mr. Wahlquist needs to be where Dr. Myers can take care of him," she said. "His kidneys aren't nearly as good as he thinks they are, poor dear. And he's got prostate problems too. I'll be glad to get back to my flowers. You can't raise nice flowers and be gone all summer, I can tell you that."

Mr. Wahlquist had been born twenty years after Custer's defeat on the Little Bighorn and had grown up on the family farm outside Redbird, Nebraska. Already as a boy he had mourned the death of the wolves, buffalo, grizzly bears, and all the wild Indian tribes. He had searched the fields and hills for buffalo skulls, old wallows, stands of unplowed buffalo grass, and rock tepee circles. Along the creeks and under the old cottonwoods, he had dug in the soil for arrowheads, necklaces of grizzly claws, and lance points spilled from tree burial platforms collapsed a hundred years before.

In the fall evenings he stood in his father's fields to watch the great grey flocks of Canada geese, which were for him one of the few wild things that still came in multitudes. He crawled along the Nebraska fences and ditches to be near the numberless feeding birds, to hear their gabble, to watch them, call them. And when, startled, they rose yelping and clamorous into the twilight, he stood up, running and lifting his arms toward the flying geese and calling after them.

For forty years the Wahlquists had spent every vacation in Yellowstone. After Mr. Wahlquist's retirement from Sears five years before, they had bought a bigger trailer and stayed all summer. They had no children. He had white hair and wore gold-rimmed glasses with flat lenses that flashed silver in the light.

When the Central Plateau herd was down, Mr. Wahlquist drove out to Hayden Valley in the early evening to stand on top of a hill to watch them until they vanished into the growing darkness. He liked evenings best. In his hand he always carried a bone whistle, an arrowhead, an obsidian skinning knife, or some other Indian artifact from his collection in the house trailer. He gave me things to touch when I was in the trailer for supper or a piece of chocolate cake and a glass of milk. He told me the Plains Indians believed the buffalo came from a great cave in the earth.

"No man ever knew how many buffalo there were," he said. "Fifty million, sixty, seventy—maybe more. The herds filled whole valleys. They took days to cross a river. The land was black with buffalo then. And when they ran, it was like thunder. Now all you can do is read about them in the journals or diaries or look at the pictures men painted then." Mr. Wahlquist handed me a lance. "Feel this," he said. "The Crow were great hunters."

"I guess they were," I said. I liked Indians.

Labor Day morning at five I left Lake for Hayden Valley with Barney in his pickup to begin the search. Steve and Mark, both seasonals, had left earlier in the truck with the wrangler and the horses. Jerry and Ralph, two seasonals on loan from Mammoth to help in the search, were going to meet us at Mr. Wahlquist's red pickup in Hayden. We needed them because we had a fire at Clear Creek, and some of our rangers were on that. We couldn't get the helicopter. Old Faithful had it on a search for three lost Boy Scouts. In our patrol vehicles we carried black plastic body bags for visitors who died or got killed in the park.

I thought Mr. Wahlquist had just hiked too far, and we'd find him tired out and waiting for us on a hilltop somewhere, so we'd get back early. I really didn't think he'd had a heart attack or anything. I had a farewell date with Marilyn, the nurse I'd been going with most of the summer. Mark had another one of his hot dates. We were roommates. He called Mr. Wahlquist Geronimo. Mark had told Barney we both had dates set up for after the search.

"Wonderful," Barney said.

Labor Day was the last day of the last big weekend of the summer. All the campgrounds and trailer parks had been full for three days, visitors even camping on the pull-offs and along the roads. But by evening all but a few of the visitors would be gone, and by Tuesday all of the seasonal personnel would be gone too, and all the concessions closed, the park left to the permanent personnel, the birds and animals, and the snow.

An early arctic storm coming down out of Canada was forecast that evening, but Barney said it would probably just blow through, spreading the fires, maybe dropping a little snow on the high mountain peaks. We had three fires going in the park. The biggest was ours at Clear Creek, across Yellowstone Lake. The summer had been very dry and hot, the big thunderstorms just blowing through, not dropping much rain, the lightning strikes starting fires.

The temperature was twenty degrees too warm for the first week in September. Some summers Yellowstone had snow every month. Every day during the last week, Mr. Wahlquist had listened and watched for the first flocks of migrating Canada geese. He liked Canada geese. The first big fall storm started them south.

"The Canada goose is his favorite bird," Mrs. Wahlquist said.

"Yes," I said.

Mrs. Wahlquist had come to the station just before midnight Sunday to report Mr. Wahlquist missing. The Whites, who lived in the trailer next to them, brought her. I walked her back to the car. "He'll be just fine," I said. After I filled out the report and they left, Barney sent me out to Hayden Valley to check. I had found Mr. Wahlquist's red pickup parked on a pull-off, but I hadn't found him.

Under the full moon, I had stood on the side of the main road and searched the tops of the blue sagebrush hills with my binoculars, dropping the binoculars on the strap around my neck to cup my hands and call, "Mr. Wahlquist! Mr. Wahlquist!" But I heard only the yapping of the coyotes and the hooting of owls in answer. When we were doing a day search for a lost visitor, Barney always told us to watch for ravens bunching up, because they were as big a help as vultures. But ravens didn't feed at night.

Before I had left Lake to check on Mr. Wahlquist, Barney had told me to drive up the Trout Creek road to the dump and do a binocular search every quarter of a mile. The dump road cut from the main park road all the way up through Hayden Valley to the Central Plateau. Barney thought Mr. Wahlquist might have gotten out to the road if he was sick or hurt. He said to check the hills around the dump.

"He might have hiked up there to sit on a hill and watch grizzlies. The moon's bright enough."

"That's a long hike for him, Barney," I said. "Too much smoke up there anyway."

"Check it out. If he's down on his back in that sagebrush with a broken leg or a heart attack, we got our work cut out for us. One of those wandering dump grizzlies finds him, he's going to get dragged for a mile, and *then* there won't be much left to find. He could've got run over by that buffalo herd if he got too close. Find the herd, and you'll find Wahlquist, maybe. It's happened before."

I did the binocular search, but I didn't see Mr. Wahlquist on any of the surrounding blue moonlit hills, or the herd. We'd had no wind, or even a breeze, so the smoke was bad. Fires, the flames low and guttering, burned all summer long at the dump; they ate back in the garbage so deep that only six feet of winter snow could smother them. When there was no breeze or wind, the dump lay under smoke, the smoke moving down along Trout Creek like slow, grey water. The Park Service planned to close the dumps in a couple of years so the grizzlies would return to their natural feeding habits.

The dump was one of the best shows in the park; the superintendent was always taking VIPs up at night to see the feeding grizzlies, although the dump was closed to everybody else. During the day the grizzlies stayed in a big grove of pines two hundred yards above the dump on the facing hill. They had paths as hard as cement beat down through the sagebrush and the high sedge. In the evening they came running down the trails to feed on the wet garbage and on the car-killed animals the road crews brought up. Six or eight grizzlies came at one time, moving down the track to be lost in the smoky haze.

We patrolled the dump road every day to keep visitors from hiking up from the vehicle barricade to watch the grizzlies. Visitors stood right at the dump to take movies and pictures. They wouldn't stand on a hill a half mile back and just watch with binoculars. The dump was one of the most dangerous places in the park; a visitor had been mauled the year before.

Visitors were crazy to see a grizzly; they always wanted to know how many people had been killed and eaten in the park. They had torn all the claws off the mounted grizzlies not behind glass at the visitor centers. Visitors wanted to know how many grizzlies wore collars. A research team had drugged some of the bears at the dump and tagged them with big orange plastic collars and electronic beepers.

Before we got on our horses Monday morning to make hundred-yard-wide sweeps across Hayden Valley, Barney told me to get in the pickup and check the dump again. He sent Jerry and Ralph out along the main road in their patrol car, and he had Mark and Steve walk along the river to look for a floating body. We'd already had three drownings since June.

"Use your binoculars and watch for ravens bunching up," Barney said. He looked at me. "Check those hills around the dump again. He could be up there."

"Okay, Barney."

"And watch for that buffalo herd."

"Okay, Barney."

I had met the Wahlquists the first evening I checked the Fishing Bridge Trailer Park as a new seasonal ranger in early June. When I saw their Nebraska plates, I told them I was from Omaha. They invited me in for a piece of apple pie and a glass of milk. Barney knew the Wahlquists; most of the permanent rangers did. Within a week Mrs. Wahlquist was ironing my shirts and doing my sewing. "It's nice to have something useful to do," she said. I did my own washing.

The trailer was a small museum. It was full of books, maps, Indian and mountain-man artifacts, prints, paintings and drawings, photographs a hundred years old, and small bronze animals, birds, and warriors. Mr. Wahlquist had collected artifacts since he was a boy. Mrs. Wahlquist said their house was full of his Indian things. He knew a lot of Crow words. The Crows were his favorite tribe. But he liked the Sioux too because they had stopped Custer at the Little Bighorn. On the trailer wall he had framed pictures of Sitting Bull, Gall, and Crazy Horse.

On the wall across from the table was a big map of the upper-Missouri country on which he'd written in all the historical notes—Indian trails, river fords, battle sites, hunting grounds, burial grounds, sacred mountains, winter camps, buffalo jumps. He'd spent forty years visiting the places he'd read about in the accounts left by the trappers, mountain men, explorers, and Indians. He liked to stand at the place and read from what had been written.

Mrs. Wahlquist had told me early in the summer that Mr. Wahlquist had started getting up in the middle of the night to walk out and sit in his chair by the big window.

He didn't read. He sat there silent in the grey light looking out across Yellowstone Lake, sometimes holding one of his lances or a bow and a handful of arrows. She didn't disturb him. I told her he just probably wanted to think. "My husband was born at least a hundred years too late," Mrs. Wahlquist said the first evening I visited in the trailer. She reached up to hold his hand. They were very affectionate. She had a large gold-framed picture of Mr. Wahlquist on the end table by her chair. She liked me to bring Marilyn when I visited, or when they invited me over for supper or just for a piece of pie or cake. Mrs. Wahlquist was a real cook.

I took Mark once, but after that he kept telling his girlfriends about Geronimo, which I didn't like, so I didn't take him again. Mr. Wahlquist didn't wear Indian moccasins, a headband, or any Indian clothes. He wasn't a nut. A lot of park visitors walked around dressed like Indians or mountain men. Some camped in tepees. They wanted to know where the Indians had camped and hunted and where the old trails were. Sometimes out in the backcountry, they killed a deer or maybe a small black bear with a bow or a muzzle-loading rifle, and then we arrested them. They really thought nothing had changed.

"The wilderness is gone now," Mr. Wahlquist said that first night. He stood looking at his wall map. "You can still find little pieces of it, but it's mostly gone." The lenses of his glasses flashed silver in the light. "Gone. It's a land of spirits. That's all. All you can do is think about what it was like."

"Now, dear," Mrs. Wahlquist said, "don't get upset."

Mr. Wahlquist handed me his Crow lance with the rawhide-wrapped shaft. He had a Pawnee lance his grandfather had found on the family farm in a cottonwood grove, where it had spilled years before from a collapsed burial platform. He had four lances altogether. "You can still touch their tools and weapons," he said.

Because Mrs. Wahlquist had arthritis, she couldn't hike with Mr. Wahlquist in the evenings anymore to listen and watch for animals and birds, to visit the Indian places only he knew about, or simply to watch the land fill with shadow. I went with him sometimes. I liked him. He gave me books to read from his library; I liked to read.

Working shifts, I had the time. I dated Marilyn, but I still had time. We weren't heavy; I had law school in the fall. Yellowstone was just my summer off. Mrs. Wahlquist liked me to go with him. She didn't want him to go alone now. When we came back she always invited me to supper; she was an even better cook than my mother.

I didn't find Mr. Wahlquist at the dump when Barney sent me up before we started the search. That early in the morning the smoke was like fog, everything unreal, the smoke filling the gully between the dump and the facing hill and seeping down Trout Creek. There was no breeze. Gulls and ravens fed on the garbage in noisy flocks. At night the gulls roosted at the mouth of the Yellowstone River and every day made the journey to the dump and back. The feeding coyotes and black bear, shadowy in the smoke, raised their heads to watch me when I got out of the pickup. The grizzlies were gone. I put the binoculars on the black grove of pines where they spent the day, but I saw no grizzlies.

The main road was almost solid with traffic when I got back down to Barney from the dump; visitors were stopping to ask what we were doing and to take pictures and movies. None of the others had found Mr. Wahlquist or the herd either.

"Maybe old Geronimo got too close and got trampled, Barney," Mark said.

Barney looked at Mark. "Maybe." Barney got a body bag from the locker in the back of the pickup and put it in his saddlebag.

Barney radioed to check on the Clear Creek fire, which was heating up, and then radioed for a patrol car to come and keep traffic from jamming up too much. Families from neighboring states saved up a day or two of vacation to tack onto the Labor Day weekend and take their kids one last time to Yellowstone. But now they were getting out through the high mountain passes before the storm hit.

Riding about twenty-five yards apart, we first swept the river side of the highway for half a mile below and above the red pickup. I rode next to Barney on the right and carried the pack radio; I listened to the calls. Madison Junction still had four teenage kids lost on a swimming trip in one of the dead geyser basins. Canyon had a gas tanker jackknifed and turned over on Dunraven Pass. Every sweep we flushed owls from the sagebrush. Three times before noon Barney called the fire boss at Clear Creek to check on the fire, which was still moving. While Barney used the radio, I sat turned in my saddle to watch the continuous dark line of traffic, moving down the long, wide valley.

All of my trips with Mr. Wahlquist had been inside the park, except one daylong trip I had taken with him into Montana to see a buffalo jump and the Custer monument. Silent, we had stood in the late afternoon looking at the white headstones on the hill. When Mr. Wahlquist finally spoke, he used Crow words, and I didn't understand. He was silent again in the visitor center until we stood before a large painting of a group of Sioux chiefs. "They should never have let Lewis and Clark go up the Missouri," he said. "The land was sacred."

"No," I said, "they shouldn't have."

In the Yellowstone evenings when we were out, all sounds were hushed, everything blue-grey, visitors camped for the night, so we were alone. Mists rose from the hot springs and geysers along the rivers and streams, and from the dark trees came the hooting of owls.

I liked the evenings too, but Mr. Wahlquist saw and heard things I didn't. He took me to see rock graves, old fishing camps, and black ledges of basalt from which the Indians had made weapons and tools. It was as if what he looked for, and the only thing that could make him happy was finding a band of Crows still living in the park, but nocturnal now after a hundred years, coming out only at night, like bats. And he would see them across a meadow or on a hill, and they would signal him to come, and he would leave me, tell me to say good-bye to Mrs. Wahlquist, vanish into the surrounding mountains.

"He'll be just fine," she would say.

Some evenings we only drove out to Hayden Valley to listen to coyotes. We walked back off the main road two or three hundred yards to sit or stand on a hill and listen. Actually Mr. Wahlquist wanted to hear wolves, although wolves were extinct in Yellowstone.

"They killed them all on a predator-control program fifty years ago," he told me. "There's no chance I'll see one now unless the Park Service transplants wolves in from Alaska or Canada."

"I know," I said. Visitors came into the ranger stations and visitor centers all the time to report seeing wolves, but they were always just big coyotes.

Standing on the top of the hill, Mr. Wahlquist looked out across the blue-grey moonlit hills. He always spoke quietly.

"Big packs of wolves used to follow the buffalo herds. The biggest wolves weighed up to a hundred and eighty pounds. They were grey, white, black, and some even red. They filled these valleys with their howling at night. They sat circling the hunting camps, their eyes red in the fire-light. Tens of thousands of wolves inhabited the upper-Missouri country." He turned from looking across the fading evening hills to look at me. "Now all you can do is think about the sound they made." The wolf was one of Mr. Wahlquist's favorite animals.

If I went by the trailer and Mr. Wahlquist was out alone on one of his trips, Mrs. Wahlquist invited me in for something to eat. She always talked to me about Mr. Wahlquist and how he'd changed. "He's more serious," she said. "He doesn't laugh like he used to. But, of course, he's not a well man. I've phoned Dr. Myers for an appointment the day after we get back. His heart isn't the best, I don't think. He knows this is our last summer. He knows. It's nice he's got his Indian things."

She woke up more often to find him sitting in his chair, his buffalo robe over his shoulders, staring out the window at the lake, the mountains beyond, and holding a buffalo skull, his rawhide-wrapped lance, or some other artifact. He used to hike in the backcountry to watch grizzlies; often he'd be gone several days. One artifact he didn't have was a necklace of grizzly claws. I'd taken him up to the dump twice at night.

"He's been a good husband," she said to me one evening when Mr. Wahlquist was gone. "He never made a lot of money working for Sears, but we had enough. We didn't have any children, of course. Mr. Wahlquist should have had a son or two and had a job outdoors." She shook her head. "If we do come back next summer, I'm sure it will just be for a week." She showed me pictures in their albums of Mr. Wahlquist as a boy in Nebraska.

By noon we had searched from the highway to the river and made four sweeps above the highway. We ate lunch on a ledge. We hadn't found any sign of Mr. Wahlquist or the buffalo herd. We all wore our jackets now; the air had grown colder; clouds were moving down from the north. Barney always said it could snow any day of any month in Yellowstone.

Barney kept looking up at the clouds.

"If we don't find him and that storm hits, I'll be out here looking for him next spring. We need that chopper."

I watched the distant grey hills. I still hoped to see Mr. Wahlquist.

A Hollywood movie director wanted to build bleachers and stage Custer's Last Stand daily in Hayden Valley all summer. There was a big natural amphitheater he said was a perfect place. It was near the main road. He said he could hire real Indians off the reservation. I didn't want that to happen. The hotels, lodges, service stations, stores, cafeterias, and visitor centers were bad enough.

I turned to watch the traffic. I didn't feel like eating. Driving out from Lake, Barney and I had passed a lot of campers and trailers parked in the pull-offs and scenic parking areas. We watched for bonfires on the asphalt. In June a visitor had built a fire on a pull-off that had just been reasphalted that day, and he had burned up his pickup and camper. Barney didn't want to ticket him, but had to because he'd destroyed government property. The highway had been jammed for a mile in each direction with visitors stopping to take pictures and movies.

"They ought to give that outfit down in Jackson Hole a contract to provide a little entertainment around here," Barney said when we were driving back to Lake that evening after the fire. "We could have stagecoach robberies, gunfights, Indian battles too—the whole works, just like they do." He shook his head. "Wonderful."

Jackson Hole was the big party town for seasonal rangers and their girls. I'd taken Marilyn down three or four times during the summer.

Barney had been a ranger in Yellowstone for twenty years. There wasn't much he hadn't seen. He said our main job was to keep as many visitors as possible in one piece and stop them from running off with any more of the park than was necessary. They took antlers, skulls, trees, plants, pieces of geyser cone, and signs. One visitor brought in a big live trap to catch a black bear cub for his son. I didn't mind arresting people like that.

I had gone with Mr. Wahlquist three times during the summer to Hayden Valley to hide in the high sedge and watch the small flocks of local geese along the Yellowstone River. When Mr. Wahlquist was younger, he had swum in the Yellowstone, but fresh from the lake, the river was too cold for him now. He swam in the Firehole, which was much smaller and fed by the runoff from a thousand hot springs and geysers. He took me with him the first week I met him and Mrs. Wahlquist.

"Now you two be careful," she said. "It's dangerous swimming at night like that right after supper. You shouldn't be going at all." She looked at me. "He just won't stop."

Mr. Wahlquist kissed Mrs. Wahlquist. "I'm fine." He always kissed her when we left the trailer.

In the growing dusk, for Mr. Wahlquist swam only at evening in the Firehole, we drove in the red Ford pickup to West Thumb and Old Faithful, and down a dirt road to a meadow bordering the misty river. An owl flew across the road. Mr. Wahlquist showed me where an Indian ford had crossed the Firehole, the old trail cutting up through the ledges, and then we changed to our swimming trunks. Mr. Wahlquist didn't take off his glasses.

Naked, except for his gold-rimmed glasses and black trunks, his body white under the rising moon above the peaks, his white hair shining, Mr. Wahlquist walked into the river. The dark water at his shoulders, he turned but did not speak, his glasses turning his eyes to disks of silver. He walked farther. The water at his neck, he lifted his feet, and, standing in the current, drifted down between the walls of black trees. I followed him. The river, already low because of the dry spring, was blood warm. I lifted free of the earth, drifted too. I felt no contact, except my trunks; the water was my flesh. I drifted, held my feet forward, balanced with my arms. Around the slow bend and down fifty yards, Mr. Wahlquist stood on a midriver sandbar. I drifted. My feet touched bottom. I walked up out of the dark water.

Mr. Wahlquist stood, arms raised, facing the far bank. He spoke Crow words in slow cadences, chanting almost, calling back the dead. I wouldn't have been too surprised to see a band of Crows emerge from the trees and mist, lift their hands and weapons to motion him across. I stood watching, listening. Above the river, a shadow, flew a lone Canada goose, its yelp echoing between the walls of dark trees.

Sitting there on the cold ledge with the rest of the search party, resting, I ate only half a sandwich from my sack lunch. I didn't eat my chocolate cake. Barney used the plastic body bag as a pad to sit on. Silent, we listened to the radio calls. The Old Faithful station was reporting a head-on collision and a visitor scalded in one of the mud pots. I was glad I wasn't coming back to Yellowstone. One summer was enough. They should just let in Indians and people like Mr. Wahlquist.

We started the search again after lunch, every sweep taking us higher up the long valley and away from the road and the line of cars. The air grew colder, the dark clouds lowering, filling the whole sky now, touching the distant peaks. Down on the main road, the patrol car had its red flashers on nearly all the time.

Driving out from Lake to Hayden, Barney and I had seen a car-killed three-point buck lying in the barrow pit, three ravens on top of it. Cars killed a lot of animals. The road crew picked up the big animals—deer, antelope, elk—and hauled them up to the dump for the grizzlies. Grizzlies sometimes dragged the dead animals up into the pines to feed. The crews helped us patrol the dump, but they didn't work on Sundays or holidays. Barney said if the Park Service closed the dump, the grizzlies would move into the campground to forage. "That ought to add to the general merriment around here." He shook his head. "Wonderful."

In July Barney had to shoot a grizzly that was causing a lot of trouble in the Pelican Creek Campground. Grizzlies very seldom came into the campgrounds. Black bears were always trouble. We live-trapped them and marked them. After the third time we hauled them out in the back country and shot them. Only permanent rangers were allowed to carry rifles in their vehicles.

Mark wanted to shoot a grizzly and take each of his girlfriends a claw. The girls all worked for the concessions. He liked to sneak them up to the dump in the patrol car, because the girls always screamed and threw their arms around him when a grizzly walked over and looked through the window. Mark told them stories about grizzlies killing two visitors. And he always blew his sirens and turned on his red flashers to scare the grizzlies and impress the girls.

If a grizzly got poisoned at the dump, or Barney had to shoot one that got dangerous in the campgrounds, the seasonal rangers cut off the front paws and divided up the long claws. I had a couple to take home. Barney always carried his rifle in the locker in back of his pickup, the magazine full of shells but nothing in the chamber.

As we searched, the hills grew darker under the lowering clouds, the mountains vanishing. I kept hoping we'd find the herd. I'd gone with Mr. Wahlquist five or six times to look for buffalo when the herd was reported within a mile of the main road. He gave me a book to read about buffalo, and he got down books to show me drawings and paintings of buffalo, read to me from diaries and journals about hunts, stampedes, men gored and killed by the great bulls. He gave me one of his buffalo skulls to hold, which his father had found on the Nebraska farm as a boy.

His buffalo robe covered his chair. He gave me one of his lances to hold.

"It was the greatest herd of animals ever to inhabit the earth," he said. "Now it is gone, except for a few scattered bands. Vanished. The buffalo was one of the great spiritual centers of life. For the Indians even the rocks and trees were spiritual. All you can really do now is think about it."

"Now, dear, don't get upset." Mrs. Wahlquist reached up to take his hand. "You think too much sometimes."

Mrs. Wahlquist told me Mr. Wahlquist had always liked to climb to the tops of peaks to stand and look across to the far horizons, sometimes staying on the peak through the night. Bitterroot, Big Horn, Wind River, Gallatin, Teton, Bearpaw, Absaroka—he had climbed in all the ranges around Yellowstone. And he'd swum in all the lakes and rivers.

"He's always been very strong until this last year," Mrs. Wahlquist said. "It wouldn't surprise me if Dr. Myers tells us he's got high blood pressure. He's got to be careful. I'm just glad he doesn't have my arthritis too."

Mr. Wahlquist liked to drive to Dunraven Pass or up toward the East Entrance in the early evenings to walk out and stand on a ledge and watch the sun go down across the peaks and ranges, see the land filling with darkness.

"The land was all sacred once," he said, "inhabited by the living and the dead. The tribes were the only men— Shoshone, Crow, Blackfoot, Bannock, Sioux, Cheyenne, Pawnee. They built no cities. They were the greatest hunters and the finest light cavalry in the world. The Crows called the upper Missouri the top of the world. The white man had to lie about what he saw; he couldn't deal with it otherwise. The mountains, prairies, and sky were too vast. The birds and animals were too numerous."

We stood at the top of Dunraven watching the land fill with twilight shadows. Mr. Wahlquist spoke without looking at me. In his hand he kept turning a Crow obsidian skinning knife, feeling the sharp edge, the worked surface.

It would have been good to see a mounted band of Crows coming up the ridge leading one riderless horse. I would just go back and tell Mrs. Wahlquist what had happened.

The shadows grew into darkness, all the detail fading. Owls hooted; coyotes yelped and cried. "The tribes should never have let the white man cross the Mississippi," Mr. Wahlquist said. "The land belonged to them."

"Right," I said.

He stood, a dark silhouette against the sky.

Barney always said that the Park Service at one time had a plan to bus visitors into Yellowstone for the day and not let them camp or stay overnight, but it had died. "What they ought to do is put in a monorail and not let anybody get out of the cars," he said. "They should tear down all the buildings, rip up all the roads, and haul it all out."

With over a million visitors, anything could happen in Yellowstone—rape, assault, robbery, drownings, fatal vehicle accidents, theft of artifacts, riots, shoplifting, arson, wild pot parties. It was good experience for somebody starting law school in two weeks.

Barney called twice to check on the fire. A heavy snow was forecast now. A beginning wind moved the dark clouds. "It don't look too good," Barney said.

I didn't speak. I wanted to see Mr. Wahlquist standing silhouetted on top of a distant grey hill. I didn't think he would mind dying in the park, but I really felt sorry for Mrs. Wahlquist.

I watched for geese. Every day for the past week, Mr. Wahlquist had watched for the first northern flocks coming down. Friday I had gone with Mr. Wahlquist to look for Canada geese. All the young were flying well now and ready to join the great northern migratory flocks Mr. Wahlquist watched for. Hidden, we lay in the high sedge watching the low-flying small flocks come over and land in the sloughs at the edge of the river. Mr. Wahlquist called to them, spoke, his voice indistinguishable from theirs. And at dusk he stood up, the flocks rising from the water, clamorous, the white underwings flashing in the grey darkness. Beautiful. Mr. Wahlquist called and called to them, waded out into the slough to his knees calling, talking.

Saturday Mrs. Wahlquist told me she had awakened to a strange sound in the trailer in the middle of the night. Chanting in low tones, wrapped in his buffalo robe, holding his lance with the rawhide-wrapped staff, Mr. Wahlquist danced in a circle before the window facing the silver-green lake, his movements slow, rhythmic.

"I didn't say anything to him this morning, of course," she said. "I fixed him a nice breakfast, and then he read before he went out." She looked at Mr. Wahlquist's gold-framed picture on the end table. "He was just born too late, poor dear." She shook her head. "I'm glad we're leaving for Omaha Wednesday morning. He needs Dr. Myers. He's just not the same man. He only reads from the diaries and journals now, and always in a whisper to himself. He doesn't ever buy a paper at the store anymore. He always used to read his paper every morning before he went to work downtown at Sears."

She invited me to come by their house and see Mr. Wahlquist's Indian things when I got back to Omaha. "He'll enjoy showing them to you. Every room in the house is full. I'll show you my roses. We've had to hire a neighbor to take care of the yard these last few summers. He's very good."

I'd taken Mr. Wahlquist up to the Trout Creek dump to see the grizzlies Monday night when I started swing shift and had vehicle patrol. I thought it might cheer him up a little. No grizzlies fed on top of the dump when we drove up, and the smoke from the flickering fires made it hard to see at night directly across to the hill where the trails came down, even with a spotlight. But then a big grizzly climbed up out of the smoke and patches of low flame at the edge of the dump, rose up on his hind legs, and stood looking at us, his eyes reflecting red. I put the spot on him; Mr. Wahlquist said nothing. He watched the grizzly until it turned and vanished. It didn't wear a plastic collar. All the seagulls and ravens were gone. The stink was a lot worse when there was no breeze.

Later, driving back down to the main road, Mr. Wahlquist asked me to stop. I followed him to the top of a hill. There, away from the smoke and stink of the dump, he stood looking down Hayden Valley toward Canyon and the black mountains, the whole lower valley dark under the moon, the Yellowstone River a wide path of silver through the darkness. Mr. Wahlquist stood silent, and then he spoke, but didn't turn to me.

"The Crows called the grizzly the great white bear and the beast that walks like a man. They danced the bear dance wearing the skin with paws and head attached. They saw the sacred grizzly in their dreams and visions."

Mr. Wahlquist stopped speaking. He watched the valley.

"A Crow hunter had only his knife, his lance, or his bow and arrows. To wear a necklace of grizzly claws was a great honor. The hunter always asked forgiveness of the bear he killed. He praised him and asked for his wisdom, courage, and strength, and for his spirit. The hunter ate his flesh and slept wrapped in his fur."

Mr. Wahlquist watched the dark valley, the moonlight turning his glasses silver.

"Tens of thousands of grizzlies lived between the Mississippi and the Pacific. There was always danger, except in winter. Now you can only read about it and think." He paused. "Animals and men weren't so different then."

"I guess not," I said.

When we got back to the trailer, Mr. Wahlquist gave me his bronze grizzly to hold. The grizzly was one of his favorite animals. At the Fishing Bridge Store, visitors bought necklaces of plastic grizzly claws. Mr. Wahlquist loaned me a book about grizzlies. I liked grizzlies. I was sorry they had to feed at the dump, but at least it kept them out of the campgrounds and from getting shot.

On our sweeps across the valley in the late grey afternoon, we cut through a twenty-foot-wide buffalo trail coming down from the Central Plateau, but we didn't see the herd. Strands and balls of coarse brown hair hung from the sharp spines of the dead sage. White buffalo bones lay scattered in some of the openings, but the skulls were gone, stolen. After the great herds had been slaughtered, the bone gatherers followed with their wagons a trail of white bones for a thousand miles north and west across the prairies to the Rocky Mountains, the bones piled finally in mile-long stacks at the railheads to be shipped east and used to make handles and buttons, and be ground up for fertilizer. The plains tribes waited for more buffalo to come from the great cave in the earth, but they didn't come.

"The tribes should have kept an army all along the Mississippi," Mr. Wahlquist said. "Everything was sacred."

"Too bad they didn't," I said. I asked him when he would have liked to have been in the Rocky Mountains first.

"Before Columbus," he said.

The next day he took me down on the lower Gardiner River to show me a huge cottonwood that had once held a Crow burial platform.

All afternoon I still watched for Mr. Wahlquist across the distant Hayden hills. Barney kept checking on the Clear

Creek fire, which was still spreading. Even at night patches of dry pine exploded in great, sudden bursts of red flame, flaring the dark sky.

At four o'clock I heard geese. Turning in my saddle, I looked up. The biggest flock I'd seen all summer flew over us in a great V, another flock behind it. I knew they were the northern geese coming down ahead of the storm, the geese Mr. Wahlquist had waited for. I watched the two flocks, their cries becoming more distant until they vanished, dark shadows against the grey sky.

We made our mile-long sweeps until after five o'clock, but we did not find Mr. Wahlquist or the Central Plateau herd. Mark kept saying Mr. Wahlquist probably got trampled so deep into the dirt we never would find him.

"Maybe," Barney said.

Before Barney started the last sweep, he sent me and Mark down to get the wrangler and the two vehicles. The whole land was dark, the dark clouds lower than the mountains, the wind cold. Flocks of gulls flew down Trout Creek toward the river. Black ravens in singles, pairs, and small bunches flew across the dark hills.

The Yellowstone River was black now. Above it, on the main road, traffic was still heavy, the last of the million visitors getting out. A California state senator who had gone through Yellowstone in June had written the Park Service a letter suggesting they give all the concession contracts to Disneyland Productions. He said they could make Yellowstone the most popular vacation attraction in the whole country. A Las Vegas casino operator wanted to put a big paddle wheeler on Yellowstone Lake for gambling and dancing; he said he'd call it The General Custer if he got the permit.

"Wonderful," Barney had said.

When Mark and I got down to the vehicles, I stood and watched a flock of gulls flying up the river. I knew Mr. Wahlquist wouldn't have any chance after the storm hit, if he was even still alive. I thought about Mrs. Wahlquist. She had told me one day Mr. Wahlquist should have been a forest ranger. "But Sears was a good job too," she said. "Good, steady jobs weren't always easy to find in those days."

One of my last trips with him, we had gone up Slough Creek to see twelve tepee rock circles at the edge of a far meadow. We had to part the high grass with our hands to see the rocks, only the tops visible now. Mr. Wahlquist stood watching the dark trees. He held the blade of a Crow lance; he spoke Crow words. I listened, watched, but only an evening owl hooted in reply, and I saw only the trees.

Mark drove the sedan back up to where the others waited; I drove Barney's pickup, the wrangler behind me with his truck. When I pulled in by Barney, he told me not to get out. "Drive up to the dump and take another look-see. This wind will have all the smoke gone. That's our only chance now."

"All right, Barney."

"And don't spend two hours up there enjoying the wildlife. We'll have these horses loaded by the time you get back." Barney shook his head. "Looks like he's going to spend the winter. We coulda used a chopper."

"Okay, Barney."

The rising wind blew the dust down along the road. I needed a hot shower, clean clothes, and supper. I wanted to talk to Marilyn and take her with me to see Mrs. Wahlquist. She'd need help getting back to Omaha. I stopped twice to do a binocular search of the hills below the dump. The only live thing I saw was a coyote. I drove up to the edge of the dump. Coyotes and black bear fed on the garbage. The grizzlies wouldn't be down out of the pines for another forty-five minutes or an hour. Most of the gulls and ravens were gone. I checked the pine grove with the binoculars and then checked the area around the dump.

Mr. Wahlquist lay in the high sedge off to the far right on the facing slope. I saw the five or six ravens first, the only bunched ravens on the slope, and then Mr. Wahlquist, facedown, the high sedge half hiding him. I stood, pressing the eyepieces of the binoculars into the bones around my eyes. The ravens were sitting on him. And then I radioed Barney. I stayed in the pickup. The ravens kept flying up, then settling again, feeding on the open wounds.

When Barney and the others got there, I showed them where Mr. Wahlquist lay.

"Looks like he got dragged a ways," Mark said.

"Damn," Barney said. "He got too close. I knew it."

Barney jumped up in the back of the pickup and handed me and Steve walkie-talkies from the locker. He took out a body bag, and his rifle. He dumped a box of shells into his jacket pocket and then slipped one into the chamber of the rifle. He told Steve to stay on top to watch for grizzlies and blow both sirens if he saw any, and then let us know where they were.

"You want to go over there? It ain't going to be pretty." He looked at me.

"Yes."

"If we don't get him out now, there won't be nothing left tomorrow but his belt buckle." Barney looked at his watch and up at the grove of black pines. Seven or eight wide trails led the two hundred yards down from the pines. "We got to move."

We followed Barney down through the soft garbage and blowing smoke. We waded Trout Creek, the cold water knee deep, the mud at the edge of the water full of grizzly tracks. Steve told us where to go. The three ravens flew away as we came up. Large clumps of uprooted sedge were black with dried blood.

We all stopped. The only sound was the wind and the cries of the last ravens and gulls leaving the dump before the night. Mr. Wahlquist lay facedown, his arms reaching out. His left side and hip had been eaten away, the bones white. His clothes were black with dried blood; his white hair, the sides of his face, and his hand were black with blood. Beetles and large black ants crawled on him. By him on the torn sedge lay his Crow lance. The rawhide-wrapped shaft was chewed and broken. The long blade was not broken. There was no blood on it.

"Well, I'll be damned," Barney said.

"He must have been nuts," Mark said, his voice a shrill whisper. "You'd have to be absolutely . . ."

"Shut up, Mark," I said quietly.

"Come on, get that bag open," Barney said. "We got to get out of here." Rifle raised, he stood looking up the hill toward the dark pines.

"He must have been nuts," Mark said. "Just plain nuts. Crazy."

Not talking, hurrying, stumbling, Barney behind us with his rifle raised, we carried Mr. Wahlquist out in the black body bag. The soft garbage came to our knees. We put him in the back of the green pickup. Mark helped me fasten the tailgate. I stood there. I wasn't sad, except for Mrs. Wahlquist.

"Look." Jerry stood at the edge of the dump, his whole arm lifted pointing toward the grove of black pines. "Hey, look."

I turned. Five grizzlies stood at the edge of the pines. The biggest grizzly, black in that grey fading light, rose up on his hind legs. The others stood up, their paws out like great hands, watching us, moving their huge heads to test the wind. Two more grizzlies came out of the pines and stood up, one with a plastic collar. The cold wind blew across the dump. All of the gulls and ravens were gone. I heard geese. I looked up. Flock after flock flew south under the black lowering clouds.

"Let's go," Barney said.

Jerry, Ralph, and Steve went with Barney in the patrol car. Mark came with me in the pickup. Barney wanted to talk to Mrs. Wahlquist before we got to Lake. He had radioed for an ambulance; it would be at the barricade when we got down.

I drove slower than Barney; I tried not to hit any bumps. Mark kept shut up. He knew I didn't want to talk, but I wasn't sad. The whole sky was black, the last light fading, only the surrounding distant mountains blacker than the clouds. I reached over and turned off the radio. It sounded as if every ranger in the park was on duty handling the last of the Labor Day crowd, helping them get out before the storm hit. The storm would put out the forest fires. Mark turned on the heater.

I stopped the pickup. Standing on the rim of a hill fifty yards away, high enough to be silhouetted in the last grey silver glow of light, was a bull buffalo. Solitary, he stood there, a perfect statue. Two more buffalo topped the hill and stopped. I pulled on the brake and opened the door.

"Hey, where you going? It's cold out there."

I shut the door.

I walked around the front of the pickup through the headlights. I walked out into the sage and stopped. Coyotes yapped on every side, the wind carrying the sound. I stood watching. Six more buffalo topped the hill, stood silhouetted in the grey light. They were moving across to Trout Creek to water. The buffalo, maybe forty or fifty now, the front of the trailing Central Plateau herd, turned darker. More buffalo crowded the hills. Standing there, my hands and face cold in the wind, I watched for the pack of wolves on the faintly lit hills. And I watched for the hunting party of Crows, their long hair blowing in the wind as they rode, in their hands the short hunting bows. I watched. The light grew dimmer, the whole scene fading, the buffalo vanishing as if into the earth itself, and on the wind only the cries of coyotes. I stood there.

Mark honked. I turned and walked back to the pickup. I opened the door and got in.

"What was so interesting?"

"Nothing." I looked straight out the windshield and down the road.

"Come on, let's go. I've got a hot one tonight if Barney ever lets us off."

I released the brake, shifted, and started down the road. We came to the top of a hill. An owl dipped down through the headlights and disappeared into the darkness beyond. Below at the barricade, red lights pulsed in the cluster of headlights, and a line of red flares burned along the highway. Headed toward the high mountain passes, a long line of traffic moved down the valley. The rising wind carried the first flakes of snow.

Dolf

Dolf stayed under, swimming with hard, powerful strokes, letting the current help him because his wool clothes, full of water, dragged him down. And all the time he was swimming, the cold river numbing him, he wanted to scream, curse, or even cry because he and Gib had been fools, hadn't done the intelligent thing. Now Gib lay in the dry grass with a Blackfoot arrow through his chest, the grass red with his blood. Dolf had heard the yelling behind him as he gulped air and went under; first they would strip Gib's body. He had to stay under, get down around the river bend and to the other side unseen. It was his only chance. He had no rifle.

When the Blackfeet had finished with Gib's body, they would come after him, sure that they had him trapped ahead of them in the long, narrow valley. Eight Blackfeet would hunt him, maybe more. Painted, some of them probably naked, their long, black hair flowing behind them as they ran, they would come after him. If he made the bend unseen, he had a chance; but only a chance, he knew, because his rifle lay on the bottom of the river.

His grief for Gib numbed his body from the inside, but he couldn't get at that now—Gib dead, his body mutilated, red with blood. Their mothers had not wanted them to leave Providence and come to the Rocky Mountains. He had to think. He could run, he knew that he could run; he had won races at Brown College. He was a good shot, but that did not help now.

Traveling at night, hiding during the day, leading the three unshod Crow ponies heavy with packs, moving closer to Blackfoot country, he and Gib had been five days off the upper Missouri when they found the valley a trapper named Wilson had told them about. White men had been in the valley but never trapped it because of the Blackfeet. The valley had a large, warm spring for bathing and washing clothes and plenty of grass and willows for the ponies. It was perfect, a paradise, just what Gib had always wanted. And they'd spent three days hidden, hoping for snow, watching for Blackfoot hunting parties, before they came down.

They wanted prime fur, and they'd found it, the river lined with beaver lodges. When the first winter storms pushed the big elk herds out of the high country and down through the valley, they could kill all the young cows they wanted, hanging them quartered in the trees near the cabin to freeze for winter. Every day they saw deer, black bear but no grizzlies, wolves, coyotes, and a few elk, and the willows were full of grouse. Ducks and geese still swam on every pond; the river swarmed with big trout.

In the valley they could trap mink and marten when the beaver stopped moving, then trap the beaver again in the spring when the ice broke. Their three ponies loaded with furs, traveling only at night, they would make the spring rendezvous on the Snake. And Dolf would go home to Providence, leave Gib, who had decided to stay at least another year in the Rocky Mountains. They were first cousins.

The valley was everything Gib had hoped to find when they left the main party, which would go into winter camp near the mouth of the Yellowstone. And the other trappers

called them fools for trying it alone that close to Blackfoot country before the deep snows filled the passes and
stopped the hunting and war parties. "You're still green,"
they said. "You'll get yourselves killed and scalped, and
tortured if they catch you alive. Blackfeet will be carrying those pretty knives and rifles of yours before spring.
They'll like your pretty white-man's hair." They turned
to Dolf. "Some Blackfoot will be wearing those city
clothes." They joked about his city clothes. He didn't
mind.

And at night the trappers rehearsed the stories of the
fights with the Blackfeet, told of their cunning, ferocity,
courage, and great skill as warriors. The Blackfeet had an
unending and sworn hatred for all white men. The trappers told, too, of the incredible untouched fur, the Blackfoot mountain valleys full of fur, the only valleys not
trapped by white men. Traveling at night, the moon full,
three times Dolf and Gib had walked through patches of
scattered human bones, all of the skulls crushed, the arm
and leg bones severed. The gnawed, polished, unburied
bones glinted in the moonlight.

Dolf stayed deep to catch the river current, but his
wool clothing slowed him. He swam hard, fought the terror in him, expecting every minute to be speared like a
fish in the clear water. He had to get around the bend,
come out of the river unseen, make the Blackfeet search
for him. He had to slow them down that much, not let
them see his rifle was gone. Only his strength reassured
him.

In the two weeks he and Gib had been in the valley,
working only at night under the full moon, they'd built
a cabin and small corral at the edge of a clearing back in
the heavy pines. They sawed the logs, because chopping
with an axe was too loud, and waited for the snow that
would give them safety. And they didn't hunt, couldn't
risk the sound of their rifles before the snow came. But

the snow didn't come, not even to the surrounding high mountain peaks, and every day the sun burned the frost off the meadow grass by midmorning, so that everything was dry.

They kept their ponies in the corral, let them graze only at night, and every day either he or Gib scouted for Blackfeet while the other slept. They built a fire only at night, kept it small and used only the driest wood so there would be little smoke. Dolf waited until dark to wash his clothes and bathe in the large warm spring that flowed into the river just below the cabin. He limited himself to two bars of soap a month; with the suds from his long hair he washed his body and the linen underclothing his mother had had her seamstress make for him to wear under his wool shirt and pants.

He and Gib had packed in plenty of coffee, sugar, flour, salt, and dried fruit, so the food would be good, not just meat and fish. And Dolf had built a shelf for his twenty pounds of books, the thin, light volumes in French, German, and Latin, and his sketching material. When the snow came, at night he would finish his sketches and study his languages. He liked the sound and feel of words. He would go back to Brown College to study for two more years, and then he would find a position as a teacher and marry. He was only nineteen; he had time.

Dolf had spent every minute he could studying the Indian languages, trying to see if there was any connection with the languages he knew, and he'd learned some of the Indian sign language. He could talk some Crow and a little Blackfoot, which he'd learned from a slave. He'd spent a lot of time in the Crow villages during the summer watching the Indians, listening to their words, and sketching.

The Crow men hunted, went on pony-stealing raids, fought their hereditary enemies, raced their ponies, played games, danced their ancient religious dances, dressed their long hair, and painted their bodies. The women did the work. Life in the Crow villages was happy; nobody hurried. Time did not exist in the Crow villages, and the only loud noise was the barking of dogs and the happy cries of playing, naked children. Dolf needed a year in a village to really study the Crow language.

He and Gib had seen the Blackfeet moving up the valley in the early afternoon, nine tall men and three women, two of the women young, all of them walking. The men all wore buckskin leggings and shirts, and their hair was longer than the women's.

"Blackfeet," Gib had said, keeping his head down behind the sagebrush where they lay hidden, looking down on the valley from the hill. "They aren't wearing paint. It's not a war party. They're probably after elk hides for shirts and leggings. They want the young cows. They don't know about us yet."

Believing the Blackfeet might smell them fifty yards away on top of the hill, hear their whispers, see them although they were invisible even to a wolf, Dolf lay next to Gib terrified. Gib kept reaching up to brush the flecks of dirt from his beard and the ends of his long hair.

Gib knew the tribes better than Dolf, knew the animals, the signs better, was better at trapping, hunting, shooting, and following blood trails. Gib was always better at everything except the Indian languages, sketching, and running. Gib had never run in the races at school.

None of the Blackfoot warriors carried a rifle. Dolf pressed into the earth to muffle his pounding heart, his body hollow and tight with terror.

"The two girls are Crow," Gib said, again lowering his head, lying flat. "Best Indian women alive, cleanest, work hardest for you." Gib raised his head again. "Slaves," he said. "The old Blackfoot woman is there to watch them and see that they work. Probably belong to the warrior in front, the one with the lance, the tallest one. Those two would almost be worth starting a fight over, one for you and one for me." Gib reached down to raise his rifle. "I could drop the warrior from here. How would you like the big, fat lady for a mother-in-law?"

The tall warrior wore his hair to his ankles.

Gib had wanted to bring two Crow women to the valley with them. He'd had them all but traded for, but Dolf had still said no. "You're a fool," Gib said. "That means we've got to do all the work keeping the fires going, cooking, and we have to prepare all the skins ourselves. Those two could make us comfortable all winter. In the spring we'd load them down with gifts and send them back to their village."

"No. I'm going to return east in the spring, and I don't intend to leave a pregnant Crow woman behind me. That's not what we came to the mountains for, is it?"

"Who says you have to get yours pregnant? She could teach you Crow every night." Gib laughed. "They don't care as long as you give them enough gifts. That's what they want. You'd have a lot more time for your studying and drawing with a woman around to do all your work. You'd never be more comfortable in your life than you would be in that valley with a Crow woman to look after you. They're different than white women."

"No."

"With all the gifts they'd be even more marriageable than before. They could both have triplets, and it wouldn't matter. Crows like kids."

"We agreed that there would be no Indian women if we spent the winter in the valley."

"You've got plenty of soap. You could keep yours clean." Gib laughed. "Those mink bedrobes are awfully soft. Yours could make you an elkskin outfit like mine. You could get rid of those wool clothes finally."

"No."

"I'll just take them both, then. We'll build a cabin with two rooms."

"No."

"Two cabins."

"No. I plan to get married a year or two after I return."

"You worry too much about your mother."

"I'm not worried about my mother." His mother's feared the wilderness. Thirty years earlier her brother had gone to take Christianity to the Indians in the Ohio Valley and never returned.

"Well, your father then. You're old enough now to do what you want. The ladies in Providence are surprised at how tall and handsome you've become."

"I know how old I am. I'm going to live my life in Providence, not here in these mountains."

"Do it, then." Gib laughed again. "So am I."

The valley was Gib's idea. One of the reasons he'd come to the Rocky Mountains was to live a winter in an untouched valley near Blackfoot country where no white man had ever trapped. Gib loved danger. The East was not dangerous enough for him.

They hadn't brought the two Crow women, but Gib found a woman in every village where they camped; he didn't crowd with the other trappers at night to rut in the high grass behind the lodges with the giggling women who sought trinkets. Gib had invited Dolf to come with him, just as he had invited him back in Providence, where at seventeen Gib already had a reputation unknown to his family. Gib laughed when Dolf said no.

"Your mother is a very lovely lady, and your father is an excellent preacher." Gib laughed again.

Around the fires at night, the great pieces of roasting meat popping and hissing over the flames, Dolf heard the boasting, the incredible exaggeration, the loud laughter. There was always the half-drunken talk about the Indian women, the comparison of women from the different tribes. And those stories finally became stories about fights, wounds, butchery, blood, death, and escape, the daily pure excitement and sometimes terror of the trappers' lives. After three or four years in the mountains, a man could be neither white nor Indian, but lost somewhere in between, his sense of time and place in the world gone. And Gib would accept no warning about that; he only laughed.

The alteration, Dolf knew now, began at the end of the St. Louis street that opened onto the edge of the wilderness. A man moved into an expanse of sky and grass plain for which he could not be prepared unless he had spent his life sailing oceans or crossing deserts. That incredible expanse began to erase all memory of vocation, family, church, and police as a man journeyed toward the mountains, where the only restraints were physical— wind, sun, storm, animals, hunger, other men, and the land itself.

Deep in the clear river, Dolf swam with strong strokes, but his air was beginning to go, his weighted clothes pulling him down, slowing him more. The bottom had to slope up soon, or he was done. He fought to keep himself from lunging up, losing all control, abandoning his only chance for life. Gib. Gib.

Hidden on the hill, Dolf and Gib had lain watching the Blackfoot hunting party move down the valley in a line; their walking had the rhythm of dance. They walked beautifully, their feathers, their skin breechcloth and moccasins part of who they were. Dolf watched them.

Gib whispered that the Blackfeet probably had their ponies tied farther down the valley, had missed the small cabin because of the heavy pines or come in above it. The tall willows, ponds, boggy spots, and the winding river made it hard to ride a pony in the valley unless a rider stayed high. Only the lead warrior carried a lance, his unstrung hunting bow tied to his quiver. The rest carried their short, powerful hunting bows strung, back quivers full of arrows. Dolf knew that such a bow could put an arrow entirely through an elk or even a buffalo. At close range it was a deadly weapon in battle.

And, lying there in the sagebrush beside Gib, his body pounding with fear and excitement, Dolf had sucked to bring his saliva back. He whispered to Gib that they should leave, abandon everything, escape on foot while they still had a chance, before the Blackfeet found the cabin and knew they were in the valley to stay. Even with their rifles they were no match for that many warriors, with probably more down below. Even Gib knew that. A storm was coming; it would cover their tracks. They had to think; Blackfeet fought until they won or died.

Gib smiled, shook his head. He liked this; he liked danger. He wanted the traps. They had carried the traps away from the cabin to the river and cached them to keep them safe until the snow came, and they could start trapping and stop worrying about the Blackfeet. Without the traps they could catch no beaver this fall or in the spring. Even if they got back to the mouth of the Yellowstone and the winter camp alive, there were no extra traps now. Gib would go without the ponies if they had to, but only after they had the traps.

But if they didn't go down to the cache, left then, at least they might have their lives. As careful as he and Gib had been, all their sign led to the cabin. They had waited for the first storms, but they got only more fall sun and heat until today, when there were heavy clouds and cold. When they had scouted down to the wide plain the river emptied into, they saw the grass fires burning, which the tribes set to increase the next year's pasture for their ponies. And Gib had daily cursed the sun. Snow would have driven the elk down to the plains, and the Blackfeet would not have followed the river up this far after them.

If they had gone when they first saw the Blackfeet, they might have made it, with the coming storm to cover them. They didn't need their provisioned warm cabin to live, their warm bedrobes they had bought from the Crow women, their ponies. They had their rifles, full powder horns and bullet pouches, tinderboxes, and knives, and they knew the land back to the Yellowstone. They could travel by night again. And if it stormed often enough, the Blackfeet would not be able to follow their tracks. Gib knew how to make snowshoes.

But Gib would not go without the traps, and after the Blackfeet had passed going back down the valley, they had bellied down from their hill through the sagebrush and into the heavy willows that filled the whole valley bottom in thick patches. Crouching, they worked their way toward the cache, stopping only to listen, watch, Dolf breathing deep against the terrible excitement in him, and the fear.

They were twenty feet apart when Dolf heard Gib shoot, turned in that instant to see Gib's whole body relax as he fell, sagging backward into the high brown grass. But the Blackfeet didn't rush them, so it had to be only one warrior who had found them in the high willows, who had killed Gib and whom Gib had either killed or wounded, giving Dolf a little time. Empty with terror, holding Gib under the arms, Dolf dragged him back into the willows and toward the river, leaving a wide blood trail. The arrow had gone through Gib's chest and out his back.

Dolf wanted to save Gib's body from the Blackfeet, who were worse than wolves, and from the heavy Blackfoot woman. He knew that Gib was dead, but Dolf wanted to save Gib's body in the river, yet knew that he could not even do that. He had to think. He had only minutes to do those things that might save his own life, at least for now. He laid Gib down. Gib's eyes were open; his blood ran from the corners of his mouth and down his beard.

Dolf cut the shoulder thongs holding Gib's powder horn and shot pouch, ran back and picked up Gib's rifle, then turned and ran hard past Gib through the willows toward the river. The feeling was gradually coming back into his body; he had never before known absolute terror. But that was mixed now with grief and his sudden and total hatred of the Blackfeet for what they had done to Gib. He needed to bury Gib.

He dropped Gib's horn, pouch, and rifle into a deep, dry, grass-covered beaver run, did it almost without stopping, yet even as he did he heard behind him in the heavy willows the yelling, the high-pitched screams, the shrill whistling.

The Blackfeet would stop to take Gib's scalp, strip his body, shoot arrows into it, slash his palms and the soles of his feet, and so stop him from being an enemy in the next life. And the big, heavy Blackfoot woman, if she came, would cut off his head, arms, genitals, and legs. And she would pound his body with a rock or hatchet, drive it into the blood-soaked earth, all the time singing and chanting, for what she did was ritual, had meaning. Whole villages moved to the battlefield after a fight to mutilate the bodies of the dead enemy. On old battlefields all the white bones were cut and broken, and no skeletons were whole.

Holding his own rifle high, Dolf had slipped down the steep bank and into the river. He had thought at first that he could swim with his heavy rifle, but immediately his heavy wool clothes and the rifle dragged him down too deep, and he had to drop the rifle or drown. And he cursed himself for a fool, because he should have pulled off his wool jacket, shirt and pants before he went into the river, for he might have made it across with his rifle then, even if he froze later.

Dolf fought now to stay deep, get around the bend, but his lungs were about to explode, his strength going. He fought the panic, terror, looked down through the clear water for the rocky river bottom sloping up toward the bank.

The Blackfeet would be confident, knowing they had him trapped somewhere ahead of them in the narrow valley, one white man. They would run him like wolves running a deer.

But first they would stop to paint themselves, all the time working themselves into a frenzy, sing their death songs. And they would shout their boasts to each other, and their insults to him, the white man, whom they had not yet seen. Some would strip naked to paint their whole bodies, the nakedness as much a part of the ritual of battle as the colors of their paints and the designs they used. They would leap into the air, whistle, make the sounds of birds and animals, and over and over repeat the sacred words to invoke their gods.

Dolf knew how little chance he had, and only then if he used his head. The Blackfeet wouldn't know he didn't have a rifle until they saw him, which would keep them together perhaps, keep them back a little at first, because Gib had already killed or wounded one of them. Yet, in the heavy willows, against their bows, a rifle was slow. A rifle was best in open country where you could use distance as an advantage.

The rocky river bottom sloped up. Dolf broke surface, stood in the water to his chest, gasping but still strong, now he had air. He was down around the bend. He pushed gasping for the shore, climbed the steep grassy bank and, out of sight from the river, fell to his knees, taking great gasps of air. But hearing in the lull of his own breathing a sound from the river, he turned and crawled back through the high brown grass to the bank.

A Blackfoot warrior was wading ashore in the chest-deep water, lifting his bow from across his chest with one hand, taking arrows from his quiver with the other as he came. Dolf dropped, fear tightening and emptying his body. He had to think or die. The warrior knew he had no rifle, but the warrior was alone, not painted, had come ahead of the others, hadn't yelled in signal, wanted to be the first to count coup. Dolf needed time and the Blackfeet's fear of the rifle he didn't have, or he would be carrion in an hour. Think.

He turned his head to look for a club within his reach but saw only thin, dead willows and the willow spikes left from where the beaver had worked. Pulling his heavy knife he flattened himself, slid closer to the edge of the bank. He had never killed a man. Coming up the Missouri, the party had fought three times against the Cree. Gib had killed a Cree. But Dolf didn't know if he had hit any of the warriors he had shot at; he had been very excited.

The trappers, men lost to their families and towns, men with ordinary Christian names, had stripped the dead Cree warriors of the clothes and ornaments they wanted. They talked to the dead men even as they scalped them, cut their throats, cut off little fingers and ears to dry and keep. They asked the dead Cree how it felt to lose their hair, have their palms and soles of their feet slashed. And the trappers, even as they wiped their knives clean on the legs of their leather pants, told stories of white men who didn't trap but hunted Indians. The number of Indian warriors they killed became the only pleasure and purpose of their lives. They tortured the wounded or captured warriors, castrated, mutilated in every way to kill, finally eating slices of human heart and liver, their laughter becoming the sound of madness. Woven into the fringes of his elkskin jacket, Gib wore strands of black hair from the Cree warrior he had killed and scalped.

"Don't worry about me, cousin," Gib had said, working by firelight on the jacket. "You worry too much. Be easy. Do you think I'm going to spend my whole life out here with the Crows?" He laughed. Now Gib was dead, the splendid Gib admired by so many women in Providence.

Dolf flattened himself lower into the grass, breathed deep through his mouth.

When the eager warrior came up over the bank, holding his bow and arrows in one hand and pulling at the high grass with the other, Dolf rose to meet him, stood with him as he stood, drove the long heavy blade into the Blackfoot's stomach, his whole body concentrated in his great desire to kill because of Gib. And at the same time he saw that the Blackfoot warrior, stripped to his loincloth, was young, sixteen or seventeen maybe. Too eager, he'd come on alone to be the first to count coup against the white man; thus he would establish his manhood and his courage and be able to boast to all the others, be honored in his village.

Dolf pulled out the knife and stabbed into the chest, felt very powerful, his free arm holding the young warrior to him, the spurting blood warming his cold hand. He felt up through the handle the blade cut through bone; the warrior's body sagged into his, the mouth open wide, but making no sound, the eyes astonished. Dolf held the warrior's body to him, at the same time dropping flat in the high grass, pulling away. He raised his head. No other Blackfeet.

His heart pounding in his chest, breathing deep gasps of air, Dolf turned. The young warrior's long, wet black hair spread over half his face and his left shoulder to the breechcloth. Blood from the two dark wounds thinned in the beads of river water. The hands lay open at his sides, palms up. Dolf felt the heavy knife. He knew what other white men would do. Quickly he wiped his knife on the breechcloth, sheathed it, wiped his hands on the grass. He turned, kept his head low, crawled to an opening in the willows where he could see up the river.

The tall Blackfoot warrior stepped out of the willows on the other side of the river, painted, stripped to his breechcloth, holding his lance. Six other warriors came out of the willows, all painted, stripped, except one who wore a fringed jacket. Gib's. Dolf hugged the ground, waited, watched. Seven left. He raised his head another inch. None of them carried Gib's rifle. He could kill the tall warrior if he had his rifle. It surprised him how much he missed holding his rifle. He liked to pull the hammer back and check the cap on the nipple, lower the hammer, do that over and over as he rode. He was a good shot.

The Indian women did not come out of the willows. They would be with the ponies; they could already be in the cabin, or the old woman could be at Gib if she knew he was dead. Dolf's whole body tightened.

The Blackfeet talked, waved their arms. The tall warrior pointed with his lance across the river. Their bodies were bright with the white, yellow, blue, and red paint.

A scalp hung from the tall warrior's lance. Dolf remembered no scalp when he and Gib had seen the Blackfeet first that afternoon. He knew it was Gib's. He closed his eyes, let his head sink onto the grass. Hate filled him, and grief. He lay there. But he had to go, to run now for his life.

He turned and crawled through the grass for fifty feet, then stood and started to run. He ran pacing himself, knowing that he would be running for hours if he made it, the longest race of his life. He had to get behind the Blackfeet and get Gib's rifle from the beaver run or dive for his own in the river. The water was clear and only shoulder deep. He had to have food and be able to fight. He had to think about what he could do.

He ran, but his heavy, wet wool clothes chafed him, slowed him, and he knew that he would have to get rid of them to run well. The Blackfeet were dressed for running. He had to run, try to save himself until dark. The Blackfeet would find where he had come out of the river, find the dead warrior, and then be tracking him through the high grass, holding back a little only because they thought he carried a rifle. They ran smooth, beautiful, and could run for hours. Dolf slowed, stopped behind a heavy willow clump, listened, began quickly to pull off his heavy, wet, impractical clothes. His heart pounded hard, but not, he knew, from running.

He had seen the Crows run down two Crees they'd captured out of a big pony-raiding party. Greased and painted, wearing horns and antlers or feathers, some naked, their long manes of black unbraided hair whipping behind them, the Crows had run, delighted in running. They ran smooth, like wolves, yelling and whistling to each other, leaping high into the air to shout and to see farther ahead, the whole village trailing them. The Crees, who had been given a head start, had lasted five or six miles down the flat, sagebrush-covered valley before they finally turned to face the arrows and the lances, already singing their death songs and shouting challenges and insults to the Crows. And then the whole trailing village had come up, the Crow women fighting each other to get at the bodies with clubs, rocks, and their skinning knives.

Dolf threw his clothes into a willow clump. He wore only the linen undershirt and pants, and his moccasins. He tightened his belt, which held his knife and tinderbox. He straightened, listened, thought he heard yelling. He grabbed up his powder horn and bullet pouch, slipping the shoulder thongs over his head even as he ran. He could have only minutes. He ran. He listened. He heard nothing. He had imagined the shouting. The Blackfeet wouldn't be across the river yet; then they would have to find his trail. He slowed down, worked to find his rhythm. Two ravens flew ahead of him.

He ran freer now, lighter, felt the air against his body as if he ran naked. He knew how strong he was, his muscles smooth and hard. He had new winter moccasins, which were very good for running. Gib had wanted him to wear buckskins.

Dolf looked up, ran, the hills rising to the endless mountains against the grey dome of clouded sky. The blizzard would come, the temperature drop to freezing in hours. Coming up the Missouri in March, the party had been overwhelmed by a sudden late blizzard that lasted three days, the winds fiercer than anything Dolf had ever known in New England, the cold beyond his comprehension. In the great spring thunderstorms the thunder rolled across the grass plains as Dolf had never heard it in his life, the lightning flashing through the low surging clouds in huge bands of blue-white light, wind a great wall, the air and earth filled with water. The trappers told stories of whole herds of buffalo caught in floods and swept down into the Missouri, the stench of death like a haze above the land. A man longed to see streets, fences, houses, cities, towns, villages.

Dolf ran, paced himself. The terror was going now; he felt a hard, cold excitement which came from the danger and the possibility of his own death, his whole body bright with that feeling. He looked down at himself as he ran; his running was smooth.

Running, Dolf edged toward the hills to get away from the swampy areas, the ponds, and away from the beaver-cut willow spikes. If he punched one of those through a moccasin and into his foot, crippled himself, left a blood trail to where he crouched hidden in the willows, he was finished. The hills were too full of ledges and rocks for good running, and if he climbed higher, the Blackfeet would see him and run him by sight. They would see that he carried no rifle. When he got out of the valley, he would carry a long heavy stick so it looked like he carried a rifle. He had to think about every possible detail or die. The valley began to narrow.

As he ran he tried to decide if the Blackfeet would guess that he hadn't shot the young warrior because he'd lost his rifle in the river. They would think that he had killed quietly to stay hidden. He hadn't taken the bow and quiver of arrows. He looked up at the higher hills. There was no cover, all of it sagebrush until the groves of pine and aspen, the bare hills rising gently to the trees. Six miles ahead up the valley, a narrow, deep gully cut down at right angles. It was his best way out, but it led only into high, open country.

Dolf watched for every rock, log, badger hole, beaver run, so he wouldn't trip, held his arms high as he ran, his damp linen shirt and pants cool against his body. He had his wind now. He had begun to sweat, the sweat moistening the dried blood on his knife hand, as if his hand bled. The young warrior had been totally surprised; he had not been difficult to kill. Dolf felt no regret, only a sense of complete mastery. They had killed Gib.

Dolf was strong; he was stronger now than when he had run in the spring games eighteen months before at school. At nineteen, he was as strong as he would ever be in his life. At night when he bathed in the hot spring, he ran his flat hands over the smooth muscles under his white skin.

Dolf felt his hair lifting off the back of his neck, flowing, now almost dry. He raised his hand to push his fingers through his heavy, long hair; he liked to do that. He had let it grow; it was a weight, which he felt now. But he hadn't grown a beard. In every village the Indians all came to look at his blond hair; they touched it. Some of the warriors wore their hair to their ankles; they spent hours every day combing and dressing their long hair. Only a

few warriors were as tall as he and Gib. The trappers had
joked with him and Gib about keeping their pretty hair.
Gib's hair was auburn; he still washed his beard and hair.
He liked them clean, light, and he urged Dolf to grow a
beard.

"Gib, Gib, oh, Gib," Dolf said suddenly. He wanted
to stop running, cry Gib's name over and over, fall on
his knees, pound the earth with his fists, squeeze his arms
tight around him. Gib's body. What words could he use
to tell Gib's mother? He wanted to kill the Blackfeet
because they had killed Gib. He and Gib had lived in
houses on the same street in Providence all of their lives.
They were brothers because they had no brothers; he was
a year younger than Gib.

They had left the East in January because they wanted
to be in time to start up the Missouri with the trapping
parties for the spring beaver catch. They had taken a boat
down the Ohio to Cairo, the land already growing more
primitive with each mile west they traveled. And from
Cairo they took another boat up to St. Louis to get outfitted and find the right trapping party headed up the
Missouri to the Rocky Mountains and the edge of the
Blackfoot country.

Gib's mother had become ill because of their trip west.
Their fathers had called them young fools, talked to them
together, had other members of the family and the Brown
faculty talk to them. His own mother had urged him not
to go, to stay and to study, perhaps to go on a hunting
tour to the Rocky Mountains in two or three years.

"You allow Gib to lead you too much, but do as you
must, son." She smiled, reached up to touch his cheek.
"Perhaps you will learn something worthwhile after all
in the Rocky Mountains."

Even now, running for his life, watching the ground
for the willow spikes that could mean his death, Dolf knew
that if it hadn't been for Gib he would never have come

to the Rocky Mountains, or to this valley. He would be home in Providence now. Gib had been fierce about coming, the wilderness a passion with him and necessary to his life. Gib had brought the maps and books to Dolf; he brought every newspaper or journal account. They went together to Boston to every lecture or discussion on the West and the Rocky Mountains and the Indians, and they saw every exhibit.

But mostly Gib talked about the Lewis and Clark expedition, and what they had found thirty years earlier, what they had done and seen because they had been the first Americans up the Missouri. When Gib was sixteen he wanted Dolf to run away with him to trap beaver in the Rocky Mountains.

"We can always go to school," he had said. "But if we don't go to the Rocky Mountains now, we never will, and the land will change. Every white man who goes makes it less primitive, and hundreds have gone since Lewis and Clark. We have to go up toward the Blackfoot country to find *real* wilderness even now. I want to spend the winter in a valley that no white man has ever trapped."

They had hunted and fished together since Dolf was eight and Gib nine. First they had gone with their fathers, but then together alone, hunted deer, black bear, and turkeys in upper New York, gone to Maine to canoe and fish and hunt, and Dolf had sketched. They had seen the Indians in the towns and visited the sites of famous battles fought during the French and Indian War. Gib knew about that war, about the Mohawk, Iroquois, Seneca, Huron and Algonquian Indians, and the white men who had gone to live with them in the great forests.

And Gib had talked all the time about going to the Rocky Mountains to hunt deer, antelope, elk, mountain lions, wolves, buffalo, and grizzly bears. He wanted to hunt where there was no end of game, hunt every day, kill as many animals as he wanted, shoot and shoot. And

Gib wanted to see the land he had read and heard about, the great grass plains, wide rivers, the incredible mountains, the endless sky. He wanted to see and find those places no other white man had ever been. Gib wanted to walk in the villages of the Mandan, Sioux, Crow, Cree, Gros Ventre, Cheyenne. And he wanted to fight the Blackfeet.

Gib had laughed when Dolf said he didn't want to kill any Blackfeet. "Why not? You're a good shot, almost as good as I am."

"I don't consider it a sport."

"Thou shalt not kill." Gib laughed. "They'll try to kill you."

"Perhaps."

After a few weeks out of St. Louis, Dolf no longer knew which day was Sunday. A man gave up clock, calendar, stopped talking about time. Day and night, shadows, the color of foliage, heat and cold were his only time, his life as timeless as dreams.

When their fathers had seen that they would not trade a year in the Rocky Mountains for a hunting tour two years later, or anything else, they outfitted them and gave them letters of credit on a St. Louis bank. Gib and Dolf bought their custom-made guns and knives in Boston, but their ponies, traps, and other gear they bought in St. Louis. Gib wanted to go with a party that rode ponies and wasn't tied to the Missouri with boats. "It's faster," he said, "and there's more chance to fight Indians and to hunt. You're freer; you see more." Even before they left Providence, Gib had begun to grow a beard.

Dolf ran. His running was a rhythm now, and he had his wind. The slung powder horn and shot pouch hit rhythmically against his side, his body unweighted without his rifle. He touched his heavy knife. A doe and fawn jumped out from a patch of willows and then vanished ahead of him up the narrow valley. He had to be careful not to push deer out of the valley flats and up the slopes. The Blackfeet would see them, and it would be almost as good as running him by sight.

A dozen parties had been outfitting in St. Louis to trap in the valleys of the Rocky Mountains that spring, but only one would trap near Blackfoot country. The party took them. Although they were green, they had good outfits, good ponies, and were young and strong, and they could already camp, shoot, and ride; the older trappers liked their guns and knives. The party would be gone two years; but Dolf and Gib, if they wanted to, could always come back with some other party returning down the Missouri the next spring or fall.

For weeks they had traveled up the Missouri, the land changing gradually from the ocean expanse of grass plains to arid plateaus. And always they looked for the mountains, looked and rode west, always west toward the distant horizon, until finally they saw the thin, low line of white which would become the looming, snow-covered Rocky Mountains. And Gib raced his pony forward that first day, laughed, shouted, yelled to Dolf to ride with him to the tops of hills for a better view of the far-off mountains.

Every day of travel had been a wonder—insects, reptiles, birds, and animals in kinds and a profusion that he and Gib had never seen before. The vegetation, soil, rocks, the very clouds and sky themselves were different, an expanse and an infinitude that changed Dolf's concept of reality, as if he dreamed what he saw. And always there was danger from floods, storms, grizzly bears, stampeding buffalo, and Indians, so that a man had to understand everything in a different way and have new emotions and responses, or die.

At night the trappers had gathered around the campfire to roast their great slabs of bloody meat, the stories repeated every night, changed, told over and over. In their excitement and anticipation, the trappers jumped up to dance, sometimes chanting Indian words, acting as Dolf had never seen men act, and he tried to understand the words. And he and Gib heard all of the Blackfoot stories, all of the reasons for hating and fearing the Blackfeet, who were devils. Blood running down their hands and chins from the meat, the trappers told Gib and Dolf that they too would leave half-breed brats behind in the mountains. All the trappers laughed. Dolf had seen such children in the villages.

"You'll learn Indian talk then," they said. "Best way is from the women; they like to talk. Those mink bedrobes the Crows make are mighty soft. Silk don't stand up to it. Why, a man could talk Crow all night. He gets two or three wives so he can talk Crow all night." The trappers laughed.

Outside the circle of campfire light each night the wolves gathered, their red eyes burning. Their howling finally became one continuous sound, the only sound except the voices and the wind.

Dolf ran, the valley growing narrower, closing him in. A doe raised her head from feeding to watch him. It was late enough in the afternoon that the deer would soon be coming out of the willows to feed. The valley was full of deer. He would hit no ponds on this side of the river, so he wouldn't be scaring any big flocks of ducks or geese into the air. He looked up as he ran. Small flocks flew all up the valley.

He was glad now that the willows still had some leaves. Many of the ducks and geese had flown south in the last two days, anticipating the first winter storm. Black ravens flew ahead of him slowly above the willows, three pair.

Running, Dolf reached down again to touch his heavy knife, grasp the handle as he had when he killed the young Blackfoot warrior. He had carried the rifle cradled across his arm every day for eight months as he rode. Always touching his body, his rifle and knife became necessary to him after that much time, changed something in him.

Dolf thought ahead of himself as he ran. He tried to see the valley in his mind, think about what he had to do, or could do, to save his life, what was possible besides running. Gib could not help him now. All he had now between himself and death was perhaps the mile separating him and the tracking Blackfeet and whatever fear they had of a rifle that was on the bottom of a river. His trail through the high grass would not be difficult to follow. Think, think. He could fire the grass with his tinderbox, but there was no down-valley wind, and the Blackfeet would only jump into the river or run up on the hillside anyway. His only way out of the valley was the big gully.

He had to have clothes, bedrobe, a rifle, extra moccasins, and snowshoes or a pony. Even if he got away now, he would die in the blizzards, or the Blackfeet would track him afterwards in the snow like a rabbit. If they had jumped him and Gib later in the day, he could have run until dark. Maybe then he could have got back past them to get Gib's rifle, if the heavy Blackfoot woman hadn't already found it, or waded into the river and felt for his own with his hands in the night water.

He could think of no safe place to hide until dark, no holes, caves, nothing. It would be sure death to hide in the willows, the Blackfeet would expect him to try that. The trappers told stories of men cringing, whining strange sounds, digging holes in the earth with their bare hands to hide, while other men fought, kept their guns, didn't give way to the horror of torture, blood, and death. The Blackfeet would fire the dry grass and flush him out. If he got behind them he might be able to run off their ponies. He could free the two young Crow slaves, give them ponies and supplies. The heavy Blackfoot woman would be his only problem, worse than a she-grizzly with cubs.

He and Gib had been fools to come to the valley, fools even to think that they could live a winter close to Blackfoot country, even if the snow was twenty feet deep. The experienced trappers had warned them. He and Gib had listened nightly to the stories of the many men who had gotten too close to Blackfoot country and not returned, men named Johnson, Jones, Wilson, Christensen, Smith, and Taylor, men always referred to by their last names.

And if he and Gib didn't return, there would be speculation, talk, until perhaps some trapper found their bones, the burned-out cabin, but not their knives or rifles. And they could report then where the two greenhorns from Rhode Island had died, where their bones had been buried, and he and Gib would become another story in the Blackfoot chronicle of death. And the trappers would tell about his taking baths with soap, washing his linen underclothing, and about Gib washing his beard and hair.

The trappers had laughed. "You boys will be so clean that those Blackfeet won't be able to smell you at all. You need a Crow woman or two to rub bear grease into your hides at night. They know what a man needs most. They keep your life simple. Beat any white woman alive for doing that."

In every Crow village trappers lived with their wives and children, had two and three wives, some of them. They always had one young wife, sometimes bought as a slave captured in a raid. The Crow women made clothes for their husbands, kept their warming fires going, cooked and brought food, dressed the skins, brought their weapons, combed their hair, and kept the children away. And the trappers' children ran naked with the other children, swam in the rivers and ponds, rode ponies, ran races, played. The Crows loved children. They stole, adopted, and bought children.

At fifteen and sixteen, when they married, the Crow girls were beautiful, quiet, graceful, and soft, with gentle, curving hips and breasts. In the Crow villages Dolf listened to their voices as he sketched them. They smiled at him and came in groups to reach out and touch his hair, touch his white face and neck and hands. He liked to sketch the Crow girls.

Dolf ran. He cut around the thick willow clumps. The linen pants and shirt were dry and light against his body now, his hair almost dry. Dolf turned to look back. He expected to hear the shouting, the whistling, hear the arrows. He tightened his flesh against the feel of an arrow hitting him in the leg or shoulder. He would fall, and if not dead, turn to face the horror. The trappers told stories of men who jumped from hiding to run screaming toward the pursuing warriors, men who, unable to endure the suspense of terror, sought death.

The Blackfeet would burn the cabin, the comfortable warm cabin that he and Gib had built at night, sawing the logs quietly. He would freeze to death, and the cabin would become something mentioned in a trapper's story. He knew that the Blackfoot woman would be at the cabin now, ransacking the place, scattering his books, sketches, and his mother's letters.

And the trappers always told how men died, killed by Indians, grizzly bears, stampeding buffalo, prairie fire; or they died of fevers, drowned, froze, or starved. Some were lost, their bodies or bones never found, their death stories never told. Around the fire the trappers lifted their leather shirts, stripped half-naked to show their wounds. And they described what it felt like to have a knife, arrow, lance, or bullet in your flesh, to know that much about death, your own blood. The trappers who scalped talked about the best way to do that and told their scalping stories. The trappers twisted the hair first to tighten the skin.

Dolf ran, ran smoothly, kept his stride even, rhythmic, held his body loose, and he watched ahead for the best path through the willows and around the patches of white, dead willow spikes. He didn't waste a step. Two grey wolves, tongues out, watched him from the hillside. He listened; he wanted to stop and listen. He ran.

"Gib, Gib."

Dolf wanted to close his eyes against the feeling, fall down. How did he tell his aunt and uncle what had happened and why? How did he tell anybody in Providence? Gib was dead, scalped, his body slashed, dismembered, the brown grass black with his dry blood now and crawling flies. He needed to bury Gib.

At the parties the girls reached up to touch Gib's auburn hair when he danced with them, his hair shining in the light from the candles and the lamps. They touched Gib's face, his strong arms and hands, which they never did for other men, and not for himself, Dolf knew. Girls left the parties early if Gib asked them.

In the cottonwood groves along the rivers, the Indian burial platforms rested high in the trees like the nests of huge prehistoric birds, the bodies covered with buffalo robes, the hands holding weapons. And in the cemeteries the bodies lay on scaffolds, wrapped, totemed, provisioned for another life. The whole land was sacred because of all the dead generations, their stories told and sung at every fire in every village. It was ceremony, ritual, religion. But Dolf did not understand, nor did Gib, who wore leather clothes, ate Indian food, and slept with the widows of Indian warriors. Dolf had seen in the language that he and Gib could never understand nor feel what the Indians understood and felt—the Mandans, Sioux, Cree, Crow, Gross Ventre, Blackfoot, Pawnee, Cheyenne.

Dolf knew that the English language had no words to tell what the Indians knew about animals, birds, sky, wind, water, earth, rocks, trees, fire, time, and death. No English words existed with those kinds of meanings or those kinds of sounds, with that simplicity and accuracy. And no white man's belief could help him understand that kind of spiritual life. A white man could only pretend, or call it superstition, or simply copy it; it was an unknowable, dangerous world to him, and alien to his own religious life.

The valley narrowed more. Dolf saw everything, had to see everything to know what he could do, think. He knew the valley. If he crossed the river and tried to get back past the Blackfeet, he would be in ponds and river sloughs, with fewer willows to hide him. They could track him easily, and he couldn't move fast. He was on the best side of the river for running. The river itself was no escape; it was too cold. He would last only ten minutes in the river. He had to get behind the Blackfeet or he had no real chance. In the river shallows they would spear him like a fish. He had to get warm clothes, a bedrobe, a rifle, drive off their ponies.

Dolf stopped. He turned and he listened, but he heard and saw nothing. He listened. And then he ran. He ran, his whole body alive to him as it had never been before in his life. The dry linen shirt and pants touched his body like air, as if he ran naked. The Blackfoot blood on the back of his hands had dried. Dry, his hair flowed, lifted from his neck with his running. He felt exhilaration now, but no terror. He ran for his life, he depended now wholly on his own mind and body to escape the seven Blackfoot warriors who would kill him. Gib couldn't help him. Dolf knew his body was splendid.

Twice he and Gib had sent packets of letters back with parties returning to St. Louis, and had received packets of letters once, at the rendezvous. Their mothers repeated in every letter how they were expected home by early fall to begin school. Men from good families had left Providence for the wilderness and never returned. He and Gib wrote only of scenery, animals, Indians, trapping, the curiosities, and Dolf wrote to his mother about the Indian languages and sent sketches.

Gib didn't write, nor did Dolf, that Gib had killed a Cree warrior, tracked him by his blood trail to scalp him, and had spent two evenings sewing strands of the Cree's hair into the fringe of his leather shirt. Neither of them wrote, either, that Gib went to the women in the villages, wanted Crow wives and would have them after Dolf left to return east after the spring trapping, and that Gib would have children in the mountains. Gib did not talk of returning soon. And Dolf knew he could say nothing that would change Gib's mind.

They did not write either how Gib had killed thirty or forty buffalo in a run, shot and shot, came back exhausted, wild, covered with blood from butchering, the great haunches of bloody meat hanging from his pony. Often Dolf did not shoot, for Gib killed fifty times more than the camp needed, was completely free to kill because of the numbers of animals beyond any meaning, with sometimes four to five different kinds of animals in view on one hillside, and eagles flying in flocks of dozens.

Gib had hunted the grizzly bears. He tried to find the largest grizzly to kill; he wanted to fill a leather bag with claws and have a Crow woman make him a necklace. They had heard a dozen times around the night fire the story of the trapper who had killed a grizzly with his long knife and lived.

Gib's eyes shone: "I would like to do that, Dolf."

Every night at the fire, listening to the stories, Gib had drawn his long, heavy knife to work on the edge with his stone. The other trappers did this too as they listened, their knives shining in the firelight when they turned them.

And the stories he and Gib had heard were no longer truth, exaggeration, or even lies. They answered, Dolf saw and knew, a man's need to speak and tell, to convince himself that he hadn't dreamed what had happened to him, what he had seen and heard. Each night a man sat eating meat by a fire in the high Rocky Mountains, his leather shirt and pants black with the human and animal blood wiped from his hands and knife. And the smell of blood from the piles of fresh meat brought the wolves, the night never quiet because of their howling.

Dolf ran, the valley growing even narrower. He kept looking at the sky to the north. The clouds had grown darker, the air no longer warm. After the snow came, if he didn't die of exposure, the Blackfeet would track him. He had to get behind them.

In the letters their mothers had urged them to return to the East to take up their good lives there again. They should not waste more than a year in the mountains among the trappers and savages. Some men did turn back on the trail, after only a few days out of St. Louis, or they went with the first party leaving the mountains. A man named Wilcox and one named Call had turned back.

The grass plains overwhelmed them, the storms, the high, looming mountains, the unfamiliar heavens, and the animals overwhelmed them. There seemed no place for white men, only animals and Indians. The Indians and all the present dangers terrified them, all of it finally the fear of death, and not the happiness of excitement and danger. Such men, Dolf had seen, did not like guns and knives, but liked groups of men, food, tents, and fires. They wanted to stay close to rivers, which led down out of the mountains to the Missouri, the Mississippi, to villages, towns, cities.

"Come home, son, as you promised, in the summer," his mother had written in her letter dated last. In the letter she told of his father's new book of sermons. His mother mentioned the names of the girls who asked about him. Dolf tried to remember their faces, the color of their hair, the touch of their white-gloved hands when he danced with them. He repeated at night sometimes the strange litany of their names.

Dolf's right foot went into an old, grass-covered beaver run, and he rolled and came up crouched. He was all right. He was by a spring. He washed his hands, rubbing off most of the dry blood before he drank, cupping the cool water with his hands, which did not tremble. He listened, he turned, stood. He expected to be able to see the thrown lance and the arrows. Having to track him slowed the Blackfeet down a little, although his trail could not be hard to follow. Peaks rose above him on every side.

He ran. He ran through the greyness, all the shadows gone. A cow elk and two calves went out ahead of him. A coyote sneaked away. A dozen ravens flew along the side of the hill. And above him hundreds of ducks and geese flew; they flew in flocks, circled higher to leave the valley ahead of the storm.

In August a storm had dropped ten inches of snow. The trappers told the stories of the summer mountain blizzards which killed men, sometimes a foot of new snow in July. But the snow melted off in hours under the blazing sun the next day, or the afternoon of the same day, so that a man thought he had dreamed the snow.

Gib liked storms; he liked to ride in storms, did not fear the lightning. Dolf had to keep working against the pain of thinking about Gib. Their families and friends could not imagine Gib scalped, mutilated, his bones scattered by an unnamed river, and not buried, the tall, strong, handsome, splendid Gib. And they could not imagine him, Dolf, half naked, running for his life, running from what had happened to Gib's body, running to save his own.

Dolf's whole family had come to see him run in the Brown-Harvard competitions the spring before he and Gib had left. His trunks and shirt were gold, made by his mother's seamstress; he had run well, delighted in running the marathon, finished fifth in a field of two hundred. His father had hugged him, his father who was one of the finest clergymen in all New England.

"You have a wonderful body, son," his mother had said. And when he turned to look at her, she said, smiling, "Mothers are proud of their sons' bodies; didn't you know that, Dolf?"

He had raced at the rendezvous in June, which had been on the upper Snake. Gib had told the whole party, pointing to him, that he raced. The young Indian women touched his blond hair, touched him, smelled his flesh. And he had won because the Indians and trappers he had run against were either drunk, half-drunk, or exhausted from three days of near riot, which for them, he knew, was both freedom and yearly necessity.

The rendezvous had lasted a week, and there had been no sleeping. The trappers gambled, shot matches, sought the Indian women, fought, raced their ponies, and traded. They feasted on the coffee, tea, sugar, dried fruit, and bread baked from the flour brought in from St. Louis in the long pack trains. And they drank the new whiskey. Men lost a year's furs in an hour's gambling, yelled and screamed, sometimes fought to the death, with knives in a circle made by other men.

And in their stories the trappers accounted for all of those who had died that year, told where and how they had died, whether killed by spring flood, starvation, fire, disease, animals, or Indians, and if they had died with courage, and if the bodies or bones had been buried. And their stories were full of the talk of the Blackfeet, the prime, untouched fur in Blackfoot country, and death, and escape from death. At the rendezvous the trapper Wilson had described a valley up near Blackfoot territory which had been seen but never trapped, and had a hot spring for soaking the cold out of bones.

Running, Dolf heard now for the first time the whistling behind him, and in a great sudden spurt of speed, he ran faster, his body tightening, emptying. But then he knew it was the echoes from the ledges and cliffs, which shoved up out of the hills now as the valley narrowed. The tall warrior carrying the lance would lead the others, coming faster now that Dolf had less room. The excitement had grown cold and hard in him, part of his center bones, that and his grief for Gib his only feelings.

Gib had traded for paints, sometimes painted his face, and one night when they bathed, he had painted his whole body blue. Gib had laughed and handed Dolf the paints, but Dolf had refused to paint his body. The Blackfeet carried their paints with them to paint their bodies with the designs and colors necessary to hunt, worship, or fight. The paints were ground from different clays and mixed with animal tallow. Warriors stripped naked to paint their whole bodies one color—blue, white, black, red, or combinations of colors, painted their ponies, tepees. They wore animal headdresses—deer, antelope, buffalo, and bear, and they danced the animal dances in all the villages. And Dolf watched but mostly listened, listened to the chanted words, the sounds that were beyond words, the sounds from dreams, watched Gib dance, his auburn hair burning in the firelight.

The big gully was a mile ahead now, and Dolf knew that he would climb out through it, because it was the only real chance he had. He couldn't get behind the Blackfeet now. If he could get across the sagebrush hills and drop back into the valley, he had a chance. He needed only a little time at the cabin. He had to take a chance that the Blackfeet would see him on the open hills and mistake the heavy long stick he would carry for a rifle. If they ran him to the end of the valley, he had no escape. Think, think.

Dolf cut east toward the gully's mouth. The gully was full of dry brush and grass to hide him once he got on the game path up the bottom, but he would have to cross the open meadow at its base. The powder horn and bullet pouch slapped against his side in rhythm as he ran.

The gully was no gamble; for otherwise he would be before dark a dead man.

He ran past a burned-out pine that had been struck by lightning, the grass burned for fifty yards around it. Lightning sometimes fired the high prairie grass and stampeded the buffalo. The Plains Indians used fire to stampede buffalo into traps that led over cliffs, killed a thousand buffalo in one place. The whole tribe camped for days to butcher and dry the meat, the women doing all of the work, the air full of the smell of blood and the smoke from the curing fires. And the naked children played among the great, bloody, skinned corpses. Dolf had seen that once, and the piles of white bones at the base of cliffs a dozen times. Hundreds of wolves and coyotes waited on the edges of the meat camps, and the air was full of croaking black ravens. The Crows sometimes fired the grass in their battles.

Dolf stopped. The gully was full of high, dry grass, weeds, and brush. He knew that. He stood there looking at the grass.

Reaching down, he lifted his powder horn, pulled the plug and spilled a little powder into his hand. Dry. Trembling slightly, he plugged the horn and opened the tinderbox on his belt. He unwrapped the oilskin pouch, river water still in the creases. His tinder, flint, and steel were dry. A breeze blew up the valley. Not a wind, but it would do if he could get the Blackfeet far enough ahead of him up the gully before he set the fire, somehow hide till they passed. The powder would help. His heart pounded. A real chance.

He couldn't expect to kill the Blackfeet, but the gully sides were steep, ledged, so they would have trouble, maybe get burned, be dizzy from breathing smoke, and have to climb half a mile up before they could get away from the fire. He would be behind them then, and perhaps have the time he needed to get back to his or Gib's rifle, the cabin, the ponies, and warm clothes and bedrobes. He had more of a chance that way than if he tried to go out through the gully. The Blackfeet could run him by sight then.

He must think. He had to keep the Blackfeet on the game path, stop them from spreading out to sweep the gully. Think. His footprints up the dusty game path wouldn't be enough; they would expect him to circle back off the path. He needed something else that would make them sure they had him, make them a little careless, as if he were wounded or hurt. Dolf looked down at the clump of willow spikes near his feet. He stared at them, a surge of new hope swelling his chest.

He ran between the willow clumps toward the gully's mouth, stopped by some scattered spikes half hidden by the grass. He rolled up the left sleeve of his linen shirt and with his heavy knife cut his arm on the white underside. He sheathed his knife and pushed above the cut to pump the blood down his arm and off the ends of his fingers onto the spikes. Bending forward, he walked toward the gully dripping blood onto his left footprint.

Still bent forward, dripping the blood, but listening for the yelps, shouts, and whistling that must come, Dolf climbed the dusty game path, the high brush on either side hiding him. Fifty yards up, he found what he wanted, a patch of dense, dry brush, weeds, and grass across the whole gully. Above that the rock sides narrowed, but the undergrowth was still thick. Once he started the fire the Blackfeet would have to go ahead of the flames until they could get onto a side ledge. Hurrying now, listening, he climbed another fifty yards above where he planned to start the fire. He knelt down. He needed something to hold their attention while he was firing the grass and brush below them. Think. He must think. Think. He looked down. His shirt. His shirt. He took it off, rubbed blood on it, and tore off a strip for a bandage. He dropped the shirt, walked up another ten yards, dripping blood. Then, holding his arm to stop the blood, he cut off the path and crawled back down to the patch of dense, dry brush and high grass where he would build his line of fire.

He listened. The steep gully sides prevented him from seeing down the valley. He tied his arm to stop the bleeding. He lay his flint, steel, tinder, and powder horn in front of him. He unplugged the powder horn. He wanted to spread the powder now, but it was safer to wait. They might see the line of powder. He would use all the powder. If he didn't get back to the cabin, he wouldn't need powder.

Crouched there, waiting, Dolf held his body tense against the terrible excitement, and the fear. If the Blackfeet all followed his blood trail, he would have time; if not, then he was done. But he could fight with his knife in the gully, and wouldn't be taking an arrow or a lance in the back as he ran, end it all quicker, not suffer torture. His body grew tighter, harder. He felt strong and had a sense of mastery. They all *had* to follow his blood trail.

Dolf waited, raised his head enough to see directly below him, gripped his long, heavy knife. They would come soon. He heard the whistling first, then the voices, the yelping and calling like geese or muted wolves. The tall warrior carrying the lance walked out of the heavy willows into his line of sight. The others came in a line spread from the hills to the river. One warrior wore his jacket and pants, another his shirt. One warrior still wore Gib's fringed jacket. Holding their weapons ready, the painted Blackfeet moved quickly, smoothly—hunting.

The scalp hung from the tall warrior's lance. Dolf knew that it was Gib's, but at that distance he still couldn't tell the hair color. He wanted to close his eyes. He needed to raise a rifle slowly, pull the hammer back slowly, check the cap on the nipple, aim, and shoot the tall warrior through the chest or stomach. It was good range, an easy shot for him. The warrior wouldn't need the Crow slaves then. Dolf looked down at his hands curled to hold a rifle.

"Gib." Dolf bent his head for that moment, pulled into himself. "The whole world was wilderness once, Dolf, the whole world, just birds, animals, and tribes of men in the forests. All a man did was hunt and fight, and he could have as many wives as he could feed."

Dolf watched. The warrior nearest the hills found the blood trail, yelped in his excitement, dropped to his knees and then stood to follow the trail back to the willow spikes. He called the others. They all talked, gestured, got down on their knees, turned to point toward the gully, became more excited. Dolf understood a few of the strange words, the language like singing. They had found the body of the young warrior at the river. They were cautious now; they would come together. The tall warrior came first.

Knife drawn, Dolf waited, crouched, hugging the earth, his terror pure excitement. The Blackfeet came quietly now, following the blood trail, not spreading out in the narrow gully, following the blood. He was afraid that they could smell him, hear him though he made no sound. Through the brush he watched the legs, stopped his breathing, his whole body pounding like one great pulse. He held his knife tight in his right hand, and he wanted almost to leap up screaming a challenge. He could surprise the Blackfeet, kill the tall warrior, maybe one more, before they were upon him, have that satisfaction because of what they had done to Gib.

Dolf counted. They all passed. He waited. He couldn't tell where they were above him now, because they made no sound. They suddenly started yelling and whistling; they'd found the shirt. Trembling, crouched, he moved across the gully spreading the gunpowder through the dry brush, leaves and grass.

Then he was down on his knees at the center of the line striking the steel against the flint. Sparks fell but didn't light the tinder. He struck again and again, his whole concentration on the sparks, expecting every second to have the Blackfeet come rushing back down on him. He would feel an arrow or the tall warrior's lance through his body, and know the horror was upon him.

A spark held, Dolf nursing it, blowing gently on the tinder. The tinder flamed, a line of fire running along the powder in both directions. And then, suddenly, the breeze caught the flames, and the gully before him was full of fire through which no man could pass and live, the only sound a great swoosh and crackle.

Dolf ran, ran free, zigzagged down the game trail and out onto the flat, hearing behind him the screams of men in agony. He would not die at nineteen, his body would not lie here in this mountain valley scalped and mutilated like Gib's. His flesh would not be eaten from his bones by wolves, rodents, birds, and finally by insects, his bones scattered and turning white in the sun. He had a real chance now to leave the wilderness forever, to return to Providence.

At the edge of the willows he stopped, turned to see the flames, smoke filling the gully. His whole body swelled with the excitement, the pride in what he had done, the joy of that. He had stopped seven Blackfoot warriors.

Suddenly a warrior appeared on a ledge high up and to the right of the gully. Dolf knew that he had been seen. The warrior raised his lance, pointed at Dolf, then his painted body vanished in the smoke that swept out from the gully.

Dolf ran, named himself a fool. He shouldn't have stopped. The Blackfeet knew now that he carried no rifle. Those who weren't burned, who got out the top ahead of the flames, would be after him again. This time they would be completely wild with vengeance, full of desire to kill him and not held back by fear of a rifle he didn't carry. He'd been a fool. Now he wouldn't have as much time. He had to have his or Gib's rifle, and clothes. The young Crow slaves would help him. He would give them ponies and food. The Blackfoot woman would fight him. He would deal with her, but he wouldn't have time to bury Gib.

Dolf looked up as he ran. The air was cooler, his linen pants his only covering. The moving, lowering clouds darkened the whole sky. Snow would come before night. Dolf ran. He pulled the cool air into his lungs, but his legs felt heavier now. He reached up to run his fingers through his thick, heavy hair. All of the ducks and geese would leave the valley. Only the ravens would stay, black and croaking against the snow. A small herd of deer ran ahead of him through the willows and then cut up onto the hillside. Two coyotes standing on a ledge watched him.

When he got back to the winter camp on the Yellowstone, he would have a story to tell, and he wouldn't have to exaggerate. It pleased him to think of telling the story. Except for the one warrior Gib had killed, he, a greenhorn, had stopped a whole party of Blackfeet. And during the winter months, sitting around the fires, reaching up to touch and stroke their long, greasy, shining beards and hair, the trappers would ask him to repeat the story in exact detail. And he would tell the story many times, but always the same.

And in the spring he would go home with the first party going back to St. Louis. Go by boat down the Missouri, or by pony or foot across land. It didn't matter as long as he got out of the mountains, the wilderness, was finished, leaving the story of the two greenhorn easterners for others to tell, and retell.

What would his voice sound like in a room in Providence, his words, in a room with furniture, carpets, his mother and Gib's mother listening? The white-curtained windows looked out to fenced gardens and neighboring houses. All of those first New England people had believed the endless dark forests stretching back from the shores of the Atlantic Ocean were full of devils, witches, and fiends. A man went into the forests at the peril of both his life and soul.

Dolf ran through the long greyness filling the widening valley. Twice he pushed the bandage back over the still-bleeding cut on his arm. Between the willow clumps he saw, finally, the dark river, and he knew exactly where he was. He turned north a little, ran past where he had thrown his clothes.

Dolf passed the young warrior's body, turned left up the river, didn't stop, reached down to grip the handle of his heavy knife. The Blackfeet had killed Gib. Dolf felt very strong. Fifty yards above where he'd come out of the river, he stopped. The current would help him. Across the dark water he saw where he had entered the river. He knew how far out he had been when he dropped his rifle.

Yellow willow leaves floated on the water. He dove in. When he got across he turned where he had entered the water before and walked into the river. He had time. The water was chest deep where he had dropped his rifle. He went under, saw the glinting rifle, extended his hand to pick the rifle up and swim forward and up to the surface. His feet touched bottom, and he walked up and out of the river. He held his rifle in front of him with both hands. He wanted to scream. He had a rifle. He turned to look back across the river. He still had time. The air chilled his naked skin.

Chilled, breathing deep against his pounding heart, Dolf ran up the bank and into the willows to the dry beaver run where he had hidden Gib's powder horn, bullet pouch, and rifle. He knelt down, hesitated, then pushed back the long, trailing dry grass.

He breathed. They lay where he had put them. He lifted them out and laid them on the grass. Quickly he dried his hands and loaded Gib's rifle, primed the nipple, set the cap, and lowered the hammer. He pulled the unfired load from his rifle, blew through the nipple to dry it, and reloaded. He tied the cut thongs and slung Gib's powder horn and bullet pouch. Holding both rifles, he stood up. His body felt different, focused, holding the two rifles. Now he had a chance to make it back to the Yellowstone. He would carry one rifle slung. The trip would be very hard, very dangerous, but he knew now he had a real chance because he had two rifles. All he really needed now was warm clothes.

Dolf turned. Between two large willow clumps, the feathered ends of a dozen arrows stood above the tall, dry grass. Gib. The Blackfoot woman had not been there.

"Where did you bury my son's body, Dolf?" His aunt would ask him that. "Did you pile heavy stones to protect the grave from wild animals? How did you mark my son's grave, Dolf?"

Dolf would come back to bury Gib's bones in the spring. One man traveling alone at night on foot could come in and get out. He had to bury Gib before he could return to Providence.

Dolf turned to look back toward the river, where the Blackfeet would cross. He knew where they would cross. He felt the two rifles in his hands. They didn't know he had two rifles. He could kill two of whatever number made it to the river after the fire, shoot them at just the right moment to force the rest to swim back across. They would give him more room when they knew he had the rifles. The fire had taught them how dangerous he was. He could kill the tall warrior to discourage them, and kill one other.

The river was the best place to meet them. He had to think about every move, hold down his hatred. He was sure he could kill two. He did not think all seven had escaped the fire; he had heard the screams. They would be overwhelmed, terrified when he fired from the trees. That pleased him. The feathered arrows stood in a cluster above the grass. Dolf turned.

Dolf ran back to where he had crossed the river, found a spot behind a pine stump and a log, and waited. His arm bled again, the blood running down his arm to his hand. He tied the wet bandage tighter. His breath came even now, and not deep. The Blackfeet would come this way; he knew that.

His wet linen pants felt cold and wouldn't dry now. He looked up. Soon it would snow. He wanted his clean, warm clothes out of the cabin. Dolf looked down at his white muscled chest and stomach, his strong white arms. He had washed his clothes yesterday and dried them on the brush in the sun and then bathed in the warm spring, washed his long hair. Whatever else the Blackfoot woman burned and destroyed, it wouldn't be his extra clothes or the bedrobes.

Dolf checked his rifles three times. He had Gib's powder horn unplugged, and extra balls, patches, and caps ready on the log in front of him. Dolf watched the river, held his rifle, forced himself to relax. Dolf's rifle lay against the log. It pleased him to think of shooting the Blackfoot warriors. He wanted to shoot the tall warrior. If he killed the leader, that would slow the others down the most. He was very excited. He would free the young Crow slaves, give them supplies, ponies. Perhaps they could travel together.

He could have made it to the cabin by now, perhaps gotten away. But he knew that here on the river was his best chance. He had to slow the Blackfeet down long enough for him to get to the cabin and find some clothes and food. Here was his best chance to kill two. He had the two rifles, and once he had clothes, food, and a pony, and had scattered the other ponies, he would start for the Yellowstone. His chances would be good then, if he traveled only at night, but the remaining warriors would, he knew, follow him without ponies.

Dolf looked at the river. Gib had wanted to bring the two Crow women. It would have been a good winter in the valley then for Gib, something he'd always desired. Dolf shook his head.

Five of the Blackfeet came in a group out of the willows on the other side. Dolf tightened, pulled his head down a little. The warrior with the lance came first. Two wore his and Gib's clothes. Dolf waited, but no more Blackfeet came out of the willows. He had stopped two with the fire. The sudden push of air from the breeze had gotten the flames moving very fast up the gully. Dolf listened to the high-pitched talk coming across the river. They were very confident because they thought he had no rifle; they had been running hard. Dolf was not terrified now.

Dolf felt the growing coldness. The four warriors with bows put them over their heads and down across their chests; all five waded in, the tall warrior first, holding the lance, the scalp tied to it. His wool jacket and pants and Gib's jacket would slow the two warriors wearing them. Dolf wanted to shoot now, kill the tall warrior, but he kept telling himself to hold, to wait until they got into the river, swam.

He had to shoot at just the right time to make them swim back, not try for his side. He listened to their words as they called to each other, their language, the strange wild sounds. He watched the five Blackfeet. By the time they got to the middle of the river, the tall warrior was last. He swam on his side to carry the lance, his long hair trailing in the water. They came closer. Dolf liked what he was doing.

Dolf waited, raised up slowly, steadied the rifle on the stump, and shot the lead warrior through the head, the whole top of his head vanishing in a slash of blood. Not watching the river, concentrating on what he was doing, making himself do it right, Dolf picked up Gib's rifle, heard the shouts, the yelling. Dolf stood up, just as the tall warrior got back to the far bank and lunged into the willows. Dolf shot the next warrior through the back as he got out of the water. He threw his arms straight up into the air, the impact of the ball pushing him forward. The fourth warrior got into the willows, but the last warrior, who wore Dolf's heavy wool jacket and pants, was swimming downstream, was too far out now to get back. Dolf reloaded very efficiently, steadied the rifle against a tree, waited, shot the warrior just as he climbed out, hung on the bank for that one moment. Hit low, he fell back, thrashing, into the water.

Kneeling, Dolf reloaded both rifles; then, not even looking behind him, he started for the cabin. Dolf wanted to shout, yell, jump into the air, scream what he had done alone, shot three Blackfeet. He felt incredibly strong and capable. No one would believe what he had done when he told the story. He had time to get what he needed now; he wouldn't be cold or hungry on his trip back to the Yellowstone, not even if it snowed. And he would have a pony; he wouldn't have to walk. He could free the Crow slaves, help them. The Blackfoot woman would have heard the three shots.

The two remaining Blackfeet would have to cross the river farther up. They would not push him hard now. He hadn't killed the leader, but they would both be singing their death songs. If the storm lasted long enough, they might die in the deep snow, freeze. He would run off their ponies, and burn their supplies, which would be at the cabin with the women. He would burn the cabin, be on the Yellowstone in three weeks, less if the first blizzards weren't too heavy. The trappers would all be amazed that he had killed four, maybe even six Blackfeet, and stopped a whole hunting party. In their stories the trappers had always told what the Blackfoot women cut off a man first, laughed, and warned him and Gib to be careful.

Dolf ran, full of a whole new strength, totally excited, capable of anything now. The valley widened; no shadows crossed the ground. The whole sky was grey with lowering clouds, some of the light already gone.

The cabin was comfortable with a fire going. The fireplace drew well; the cabin wasn't smoky. Every night he had gone down to the warm spring to bathe. It was a big spring. He only used soap once a week. Some nights Gib had gone with him. Dolf did not want to burn the comfortable cabin.

When they had first seen the hunting party that morning and the two young Crow women, Gib had said, "You need somebody to scrub your back every night, Dolf, don't you?"

Dolf ran. He knew every tree now as he got closer to the cabin. He ran, pleased with how well he'd run, how strong he was, how well he'd shot. He wished Gib had been there watching him.

Later, moving quietly, crouched, he stopped in the heavy pines at the edge of the cabin clearing. Indian ponies stood tied in the clearing and back in the trees behind the cabin. His and Gib's ponies stood in the corral. Everything from inside the cabin lay in the yard—his packages of sketches, his mother's letters, the food, his books, the soap. The clothes, sleeping robes, and cooking pots had been gathered in a pile. The tall Blackfoot woman came out of the cabin. She carried a hatchet; she kept looking toward the trees where he stood hidden. Then Dolf saw the two young Crow women sitting together back in the trees. They looked like sisters, one fifteen, the other maybe sixteen.

Dolf waited. He saw no other warriors. The girls were clean and beautiful.

Dolf stepped out into the small clearing. The young Crow women saw him first, stood up, but said nothing. The big Blackfoot woman saw him then, and with a scream of rage she ran awkwardly toward him, the hatchet raised, her voice one continuous sound. Dolf set down Gib's rifle, sidestepped her, even as he did, swinging his rifle hard by the barrel to smash the stock against the back of her skull with his full strength. She fell without a sound, lay on her face without moving.

Dolf checked the rifle stock to see that it wasn't split. He wiped the blood off with a handful of dry grass. He cocked the rifle to check the mechanism and to see that the cap still rested on the nipple.

He turned to the two young women and spoke to them in Crow. They said nothing. He told them to step closer to him. Holding his rifle across his naked chest, he asked them who they were. His words simple, he told them that he was their friend, a friend to the Crow, that he had visited many times in the Crow villages, and they didn't have to be afraid. He would help them. He reached out and touched each of them on the shoulder to reassure them. They began to talk. They said that they were slaves of the tall warrior. Dolf asked if there were more Blackfeet, and they said yes but many days away.

Dolf looked at them closely; their clothes and long hair were very clean. They were slim and beautiful, with beautiful dark eyes. Indian women matured faster than white women. In the villages they married at fourteen, some of them. Dolf had seen them, naked to the waist, nursing babies at fifteen from their full breasts. Trappers traveled long distances and traded very high to get Crow women for wives.

Dolf turned to look behind him at the border of trees, where the two warriors would come. If it were open country, prairie, the two of them would have little chance against his rifles. But as long as they were in the valley, the cover thick and the fighting at close range, he had no advantage.

He had to think quickly, decide what to do. He looked at the cabin. He didn't want to burn the cabin.

The two Blackfeet would have to come for ponies, food, and robes or they could not follow him far in the coming storm and cold. The storm might last for days. The warriors could not return to their village and say that one white man had killed so many of them. They had to kill him, and knowing that gave him an advantage.

Dolf looked at the two young women again. Their hair glistened. They could cut grass for the ponies, prepare the beaver pelts, cook, keep the cabin clean, give him time to read, study languages and sketch. They would like the hot spring.

He felt very strong, very sure of himself; his whole body was filled with heat, warmth, and pure mastery. He knew that he had done very well, better even than Gib could have done. He looked up. It was a winter sky. Soon a wind would come. The mountain passes would fill with snow, and the valley would be isolated until spring. He could bury Gib's body decently.

He turned from the two young Crow women to look at the circle of trees. He had a very good chance to kill the tall warrior if he could get the two Blackfeet to come into the clearing. After the storm was over, he could track down the other warrior in the snow. He would be easy to kill. The valley opened up, and the cover vanished lower down. He could catch him there. Without a pony and in open country, the warrior would have little chance against him with only his bow. The other Blackfeet would not come to look for the vanished hunting party until the deep snows melted in the spring.

The cabin would be comfortable all winter with the Crow women. They could teach him the language in great detail, make him clothes of elkskin. Even with a pony, food, sleeping robes, and a rifle, it would be very dangerous trying to get back to the winter camp on the Yellowstone through the blizzards and heavy snow.

It pleased and excited him to think how surprised the trappers would be when he suddenly appeared in the spring with all those furs, after they had all thought he and Gib had both been killed. He would have great stories to tell.

He would give the furs and the ponies to the young Crow women and send them with a guide back to their village. He would buy them each a new rifle at the rendezvous as a gift for their new husbands. After that he would go home to Providence. Children were always happy in the Crow villages. Dolf watched the trees. He would be able to bury Gib right. He could tell Gib's mother. He would sit in chapel and hear his father preach Gib's memorial sermon.

He picked up Gib's rifle and turned back to the young Crow women. Holding up both rifles, gesturing, he told them to drive the ponies into the trees and stay in sight at the cabin door. The ponies would not go far. The two Blackfeet would think he'd come and gone. He looked down at the dead woman. They would see her body. Dolf walked to a pile of logs he and Gib had dragged in for firewood but hadn't cut yet and crouched down. He checked both rifles. He tightened the bandage on his cut, which still bled down over his palm.

He waited, watched the edge of the clearing for movement. A breeze lifted the edges of his sketches from the ground. He chilled in his damp linen pants. He turned to watch the Crow women enter the cabin. They would fix the cut on his arm.

When his legs began to cramp, Dolf stretched them one at a time, but he did not take his eyes from the trees. He knew that he could have been gone by now, taken food and sleeping robes, gotten his clothes, scattered the ponies he didn't need, taken the Crow women with him. Perhaps he'd been a fool to try this, but as long as he had to fight the two warriors, it was better to do it here. Dolf turned once to look at the two young Crow women. They did not look at him.

Something moved at the far end of the clearing. He watched, his body tightening, the hot excitement spreading from the center of his chest into his whole body. First the tall warrior and then the other one stepped just to the edge of the trees. They watched, didn't move. The smaller warrior carried a bow; he held arrows in his right hand. The tall warrior held the lance. The scalp was tied a third of the way down the shaft.

Dolf tightened.

The tall warrior stepped back into the trees. The smaller man didn't move; he watched the cabin and empty corral. He turned his head to look at the dead Crow woman. Dolf raised his rifle slowly, laid it across the log, aimed carefully at the warrior's chest and squeezed the trigger slowly, felt the push of the rifle even as he watched the man fall backward. The man, kicking with one leg, rose to his knees, then fell forward and lay still. He had made no sound that Dolf could hear. Kneeling, Dolf reached for Gib's rifle. He should have shot the other warrior when he'd first stepped out. He should have been ready, been thinking, but at least he'd killed one.

He watched the trees; nothing moved. The tall warrior had not charged him screaming his death song. Dolf knew that, back in the trees, the tall warrior watched him. Dolf turned. He looked at the cabin. His blood beat at him. He stood up. He was very strong, masterful.

Dolf stepped out from behind the logs. He held himself very straight, cradled Gib's rifle tight in his arm, his hand on the stock. Each step deliberate, he walked out into the clearing. He knew that the tall warrior had an unstrung bow tied to his quiver. Dolf wanted to shout and chant words he didn't even know, to jump and dance. He had great strength. He did not turn to look back toward the cabin again. He walked toward the center of the clearing.

He knew that the warrior waited back in the trees. Raising his rifle, Dolf shouted in Crow and what little Blackfoot he knew, asked him if he were an old woman, if he were afraid to die, shouted that it must be lies that the Blackfeet had great courage.

"You must go gather wood with the women when you return to your village, for you are afraid of death! I have killed all of your friends; you cannot be too hard to kill! You must go back to your village and tell of your defeat by one white man! But then perhaps you will die in the coming storm and not have to return in shame!"

The tall warrior stepped out just to the edge of the trees. Dolf's whole body pounded with his hot blood, his excitement so intense he needed to scream. Dolf raised his rifle and aimed at the chest. The warrior raised his lance and hurled it hard into the ground halfway between himself and Dolf and then pulled his knife. He held it high.

Yelling words Dolf didn't understand, the warrior ran toward him across the opening. Dolf held the rifle aimed on him. Dolf saw the auburn scalp tied to the lance.

Dolf screamed even before he fired Gib's rifle into the air, set it down and drew his heavy knife. His whole body wanted to feel through the knife handle the blade going into the warrior's chest and cutting bone. Knife held out, the scream dying now, Dolf ran toward the man. They met, circled, stabbing and slashing at each other with their long heavy knives, both of them silent.

Dolf breathed through his mouth, pulled back a little. The dark, wide eyes watched him, the lips pulled back from the white teeth. Heat seemed to come from the body. The shoulders and arms were heavier than Dolf had thought.

It had grown darker.

They closed, the warrior kicked out with his feet, trying to trip Dolf. And in that instant, each grabbed the wrist of the other's knife hand, and they fell rolling, kneeing at each other, fighting with their legs. Dolf felt the hard muscles of the other man against his body, the long hair. The hand held his wrist to keep his knife back. They rolled over a hump of rock, knelt, stood slowly, pushing at each other with their knives, trying to overcome each other's strength.

Dolf sucked air through his mouth. His cut had begun to bleed, the blood running over his hand, making the warrior's wrist slick, harder to hold. Dolf pushed in with his knife, tried desperately to break the hold. He saw the smeared paint on his arms. He wanted to stab his knife deep into the warrior's body, wanted to see the warrior's whole body go lax, begin to sink, Dolf feeling the knife go in.

Dolf lunged against him, tried to bring his knife straight in, concentrated everything on that, pushed the warrior's arm up, his knife above Dolf's head. And in that instant Dolf's hold on the blood-wet wrist slipped, and he felt the blade brought down across his naked back. He screamed, grabbed for the raised arm, dropped his own knife to grab with both hands, but already feeling his own weakness. And the warrior pulled his knife back, lunged in, and Dolf felt his whole body pull into the center of his stomach where the knife hit him, his strength gone.

"No," he whispered, "no." The knife struck him in the stomach again. Falling, he hit on his side, so that he saw the high, grey mountains for that moment when he still had vision. Through the dark he heard the man scream words, the scream becoming a chant. He felt his long hair being twisted, tightened, his head lifting from the ground. He did not understand the words.

Douglas H. Thayer